**"Some people might think that you know me,"
Lachlan quipped over his shoulder and threw
her a wink.**

Iris hurried along to the changing room, then closed
the door behind her and leaned against it. Her heart
was clamoring in her chest. Tears brimmed in her eyes.
This was ridiculous. Ludicrous. They'd had a fairly
normal couple of weeks working together. Her heart
told her they were on their way to being friends. They
were even beginning to joke around with each other.
But all the stuff that she'd kept deep down inside her
for years was trying to push its way to the surface.

No. No. Iris took some deep breaths and started to
think rationally. She pressed her hand against her still-
beating-too-fast heart. Life had taken them in different
directions. Yes, she'd missed his company, his love and
the life they'd had together. But she couldn't go back.
They couldn't go back.

Dear Reader,

Marriage-reunited stories are the toughest to write because there has to be a really good reason why two people split in the first place, then another really good reason for them to take the step to potentially put themselves through heartache again.

For Lachlan and Iris there was a lot to unpack, and setting this story in beautiful Dublin made me want to take advantage of the surroundings, too.

Here's hoping you can see the deep love that has lasted for years between this pair and want them to find their happy-ever-after again. I know I did!

Love,

Scarlet

MARRIAGE MIRACLE IN EMERGENCY

SCARLET WILSON

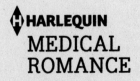

HARLEQUIN

MEDICAL
ROMANCE

HARLEQUIN®
**MEDICAL
ROMANCE**™

Recycling programs
for this product may
not exist in your area.

ISBN-13: 978-1-335-40901-0

Marriage Miracle in Emergency

Copyright © 2021 by Scarlet Wilson

This edition published by arrangement with Harlequin Books S.A.

For questions and comments about the quality of this book,
please contact us at CustomerService@Harlequin.com.

Harlequin Enterprises ULC
22 Adelaide St. West, 41st Floor
Toronto, Ontario M5H 4E3, Canada
www.Harlequin.com

Printed in U.S.A.

Scarlet Wilson wrote her first story aged eight and has never stopped. She's worked in the health service for twenty years, having trained as a nurse and a health visitor. Scarlet now works in public health and lives on the West Coast of Scotland with her fiancé and their two sons. Writing medical romances and contemporary romances is a dream come true for her.

Books by Scarlet Wilson

Harlequin Medical Romance

The Christmas Project

A Festive Fling in Stockholm

Double Miracle at St. Nicolino's Hospital

Reawakened by the Italian Surgeon

Changing Shifts

Family for the Children's Doc

London Hospital Midwives

Cinderella and the Surgeon

The Good Luck Hospital

Healing the Single Dad's Heart
Just Friends to Just Married?

His Blind Date Bride

Visit the Author Profile page
at Harlequin.com for more titles.

This story has to be dedicated to my good friend
and Dublin expert, Daisy Cummins.
Thank you, Daisy! Raising a glass to
the next time we can get together with
Heidi, Fiona and Iona too. xx

CHAPTER ONE

IRIS CONWAY PUSHED her blonde hair back from her face and yanked at her ponytail band, trying to push it all back into something more reasonable. The stained scrubs were tossed into the nearest laundry basket as she pulled a new set from the trolley in the corner of the changing room. This was the third set she'd worn on this shift so far. Things were not going well.

She shoved her feet into her shoes and elbowed her way back out the door into the noise and bedlam of the A&E department.

St Mary's University Hospital in Dublin was currently in chaos and she hated it. They were four doctors down. Two were on maternity leave, her Spanish colleague had just returned home due to some bad news and a fourth had been involved in an accident on a rugby pitch which had resulted in some emergency surgery. She strode down the corridor and glanced at the board. Every time a space appeared, it was immediately filled. They'd long since breached their four-hour waiting time.

'Rena,' she said sharply, 'I need an update.'

Rena—the charge nurse on duty—appeared at her side, her face pinched. 'X-ray is still backed up, we have six patients waiting for a medical review, three at Surgical, the paediatrician has just appeared—she's got four to review—and there's four patients waiting for casts.' Iris didn't get a chance to talk. 'The two in Resus need your attention again. I have a woman requiring an ultrasound—apparently Obstetrics are just too busy to get here. And Harry's back again. I've just made him a cup of tea and some toast. Oh, and the new doc? She's not coming any more. We're getting some guy—can't even remember his name—instead.'

Iris swallowed down her frustration. Rena looked ready to snap at the next person to say a word to her—not good news for anyone in this department. After a few days of storms, the hospital was full to bursting. There were absolutely no beds left, which was why each speciality was having trouble getting to A&E to review their patients.

Harry was one of their frequent flyers. An elderly man who'd slept in Dublin doorways for years. He never accepted any offer of accommodation, but frequented their department at least twice a week. He would likely be the only individual today that wouldn't hear the sharp end of Rena's tongue. 'Also,' she added, 'one of our new medical students is crying in the staff room, and the other needs to be gagged and handcuffed—thinks he's already qualified and can make decisions.'

Iris sighed. Just what she needed. As a university hospital, St Mary's had more than the average share of student doctors, all at varying stages of their careers. Proper supervision was difficult when she was four doctors down. 'What's she crying about?'

'No idea,' said Rena. 'I haven't had time to find out.'

Iris pressed her lips together. Comforting and investigating why a medical student was in tears would take time she simply didn't have right now—not when the department was like this—and she absolutely hated herself for it. 'Put Joan on our over-ambitious medical student. Tell him he can't do anything without her say-so.'

Joan was one of their fiercest nurse practitioners. Iris didn't usually assign students to her—mainly because they didn't seem to come out of the experience unscathed. But the last thing she needed right now was someone making a mistake. Joan would ensure that wouldn't happen.

Rena raised one eyebrow. 'You'll pay for that,' she said knowingly. Joan was the only other member of staff in here that could give Rena a run for her money.

Iris nodded. 'Oh, I know. And ask Fergus to deal with the other student.' At least he was a safe choice. Fergus, an experienced staff nurse, practically had the word *nice* hanging above his head. He could deal with any upset member of staff in an instant.

That was one of things she loved about this place. She knew the people here like family. In fact, for the last six years they had been her family. Some A&E departments were notorious for their transient staff. It was a high-stress, high-paced environment and people frequently moved on. Many doctors spent a few years in A&E for their CVs, then quickly moved on to other places. Only a few stayed the distance, and Iris was one of them. When she'd been promoted to head of department here, her surrounding colleagues had been quick to congratulate her. She'd fitted in well. Loved the city and loved the people since her arrival six years previously. When she'd adopted her daughter, Holly, on her own, they'd all had her back whenever she'd needed help at short notice. In turn, Holly loved them all, and had tough-nosed Rena and Joan, and soft-hearted Fergus, all dancing to whatever tune she played. These people were worth their weight in gold, and Iris valued every one of them. Her own adoption experience as a child hadn't been good, so she was even more determined to be the best parent she could be to her daughter.

The phone rang next to them and Iris picked it up. Her skin chilled as she listened quietly. She said a few words in acknowledgement, then replaced the phone. Rena knew instantly that something was wrong. Iris pressed the alert on her pager. 'Incoming sea rescue. Four casualties,' she said.

'We need to clear Resus,' said Rena instantly. Iris took a quick glance around the room, hearing the sounding of pagers all around her as staff received the alert.

She strode down the corridor, shouting instructions to faces that appeared from behind curtained cubicles. No one argued. All just giving a nod in agreement and disappearing again.

Part of their earlier conversation struck a chord in her head. 'What happened to our new doc—Claire somebody? Why isn't she coming?'

Rena shrugged. 'She got a better offer apparently. Some hospital in Rio de Janeiro.' She gave Iris a rueful smile. 'Don't think we can put up a fight against their weather, can we?'

Iris shook her head. 'This storm isn't helping anyway. Three days of relentless rain and gale force winds. Why does no one listen to the weather warnings and stay inside? Feels like half of Dublin is currently in our waiting room.'

'Yeah,' agreed Rena, glancing towards the packed room, with steamy windows. Every seat was taken, with plenty of others standing around inside. 'And virtually no doctors to treat them.' The irony dripped from her voice.

It seemed that no doctor on the entire Planet Earth wanted a short-term contract in their A&E department right now. Ridiculous. This was a marvellous place—or at least, it normally was.

She spent the next few minutes stabilising both patients in Resus, and getting them sent on to the A&E combined assessment unit. It was literally only supposed to be used to keep patients overnight while they awaited more tests. Both of these patients should be in beds in the wards upstairs—but Iris didn't have time to wait for that to be sorted. She picked up the nearest phone, paging the doctor on call for the medical wards.

She didn't waste any time when he answered. 'You have six patients in my department—all of whom have breached their waiting time. Get down here, review them and make a clinical decision. I have four fishermen being winched from the Irish Sea and I don't have space for them all.' She put the receiver down before he had a chance to speak.

Iris glanced at the board again and gave a quick look at her watch, making an instant decision. 'Can you get me a foetal monitor?' she asked Rena. 'That poor woman's waited long enough.'

Rena nodded and appeared a few moments later passing over the handheld monitor. Iris sucked in a deep breath and took a quick glance at the chart, then disappeared behind the curtains.

The middle-aged woman was pale-faced, with streaked mascara around her eyes. Her hair was plastered to her head. She'd come in a few hours ago reporting reduced foetal movement. She was on her own, and Iris was immediately concerned about the potential for delivering bad news to someone with no support. She knew immediately that no woman this far on in her pregnancy would have come out in this weather unless she was really worried.

She started washing her hands. 'Hi, Carrie, I'm Iris, one of the A&E consultants. I'm sorry you've had a bit of a wait, but it seems our obstetricians are caught up today. Would you mind if I looked after you instead?'

Carrie gave a quick shake of her head, her hands placed protectively over her stomach. 'I just want someone to tell me if everything is all right.'

Iris nodded and sat down next to the bed. 'I get that. Okay, I see you reported reduced movement. Can you tell me what's been happening?'

Carrie sniffed. 'I feel terrible. I hadn't even realised at first. It was just when I was walking around the supermarket earlier—when the wind dropped for a bit—and I saw someone else with a newborn strapped to their chest, and I realised I hadn't felt any movement today.'

Tears started to flow again. 'I know I felt her last night. Because she woke me up. Kicking like anything when the rain was battering off the windows. But I usually feel her most of the time. And it wasn't until then I realised I hadn't felt anything since then. And I'm an older first-time mum, and I know I'm at higher risk of everything. But all of my tests have been fine; in fact, everything's been fine, up to now.' Her words had just seemed to spill out, and they came to an abrupt halt.

There were lots of things she could say right now. But Iris knew there was only one thing this woman wanted to know.

She held up the Doppler. She spoke slowly

and clearly. 'Okay, I'm going to use this to see if we can hear baby's heartbeat. You'll have had this done before?'

Carrie nodded. 'My midwife has used it before. I phoned her today. But she was stuck out on some country road where the storms had made a tree fall. She couldn't get to me and told me to come into hospital and get checked out.'

Which was exactly the advice Iris would have expected her to give her patient. She already knew that the community midwife had phoned in to see how Carrie was, and she made a mental note to try and check up later that the midwife had got back to her base safely. 'This is the one I have immediate access to, so we'll use it first. I want to reassure you, if we don't pick up a heartbeat straight away, not to panic. Sometimes babies lie in an awkward position. Is someone with you?'

Iris knew at this stage she should always be able to pick up a heartbeat, but wanted to hedge her bets for a few more moments.

Carrie shook her head. 'It's just me. Me and Ruthie. That's what I'm going to call her.' She smiled at her belly as she stroked it. 'I never thought I could have children. Tried for years. My husband left me, then I met someone else for a while, and that didn't work out either. Then, out of the blue—' she gave a little smile

'—this. But the father didn't want to know. I knew straight away this was my last chance to be a mum and I didn't care about anything else. I don't need a man to do this. I have a good enough job and my own place. My mum and sister-in-law will help out. They were both delighted for me. But I didn't want to tell them about this. I didn't want to scare them.' She blinked, frightened eyes connecting with Iris's. 'I'm forty-four. I thought when I passed all the crucial points I was safe. Twelve weeks. Twenty weeks and the detailed scan. Then, twenty-four weeks. I thought I'd made it past all the bad stuff.' Her voice started to shake. 'I mean, this is supposed to be the final bit. The bit where you just get bigger and bigger and wait for the main event.'

Iris reached out and squeezed Carrie's hand. Empathy was washing all over her. Carrie was forty-four and thirty-five weeks pregnant with a much-wanted baby. She'd already named her little girl and made plans to do this on her own. Some of the things that she'd said struck a chord with Iris—on a personal level that she would never normally reveal to a patient. Her heart gave an unconscious twist in her chest. She really, really didn't want to give bad news to this woman today. She tempered the swelling rage in her chest that the obstetricians hadn't prioritised her. They could well be dealing with some emergencies, but Iris was well aware of the fact that in a few minutes her own attentions would be urgently needed elsewhere.

She lifted the tube of gel and showed it to Carrie. 'I need to squeeze a little of this on your stomach.'

Carrie pulled up her maternity top, revealing her pale skin with some stretch marks and Iris squeezed the gel out. Using the transducer, she spread the gel across Carrie's stomach, holding the monitor in her other hand. She flicked the switch and held her breath.

Almost immediately there was the sound of a rapid heartbeat. Iris couldn't stop the immediate smile that appeared on her face. Carrie gave an audible sigh of relief and her whole body seemed to relax. 'Ruthie,' she breathed.

'Ruthie.' Iris nodded. She moved the transducer a little, watching her black and white screen. The portable ultrasound monitors in the A&E department weren't quite top of the range, but they were certainly good enough for their purpose. She held it steady for a full minute, letting Carrie savour the sound of the heartbeat. 'Everything is in normal ranges,' she said reassuringly. 'Ruthie's heartbeat. Your blood pressure that our nurse took earlier, and the urine sample that you gave just after you arrived.'

'So, I don't need to worry?' Carrie's eyes were wide.

'Everything looks good,' said Iris. 'Do you mind if I get you booked into the maternity hospital for a review tomorrow?' She put her hand back over Carrie's. 'Only because their doctor didn't manage to see you today. I can't find anything to worry about, but we'll give you a chart to complete about foetal movement, and they can have another look at you tomorrow to make sure that they are happy too.'

Carrie looked a little wary. 'You're sure there's nothing wrong?'

Iris nodded. 'I am. I'm a very experienced A&E doctor. All your tests are normal. But I'm not your obstetrician, and if I was, and one of my patients had an A&E visit, I'd want to see them for myself.'

This seemed to make sense to Carrie, and she breathed out slowly. 'Okay, then.' Iris wiped the gel from Carrie's stomach. 'Give me five minutes and one of my staff will come back with the details. But look after yourself, Carrie. And good luck with Ruthie. She'll be in great hands.'

This time it was Carrie who reached out and grabbed Iris's hand. 'Thank you,' she breathed. 'I was so scared when I came in today. You've no idea how relieved I am.'

'I get it.' Iris smiled. 'And I'm glad we were able to help.'

She pulled back the curtain and walked quickly to the desk, giving instructions to one of her colleagues to make the appointment for Carrie and make sure she got home safely.

The thump-thump of the helicopter sounded overhead. Iris could feel the flip inside her stomach—that familiar apprehension over what might lie ahead. All she knew was that a fishing boat had overturned due to the storm and all four crew had been in the sea. She didn't even know yet if all four had been successfully winched to safety. There must have been at least two rescue helicopters out there, and doubtless some of the life craft crew too. All of those personnel would have been exposed to the cruel elements currently battering Dublin.

She could well have more than four critical patients to deal with.

'Everyone ready?' she gave a shout to the staff. It was the oddest thing. Voices quietened in the usually buzzing department. Iris could see that the two patients in Resus had been moved and the trolleys prepared. Two of the other medical patients had disappeared too, leaving two empty bays directly next to Resus.

Emergency trolleys were ready, staff were aproned, gloved and masked. Rena had bags of saline and glucose in the warmers and warming blankets prepared—standard procedures for any unit receiving potentially hypothermic patients.

There was still some background noise, but she could feel the buzz in the air. The hush only emphasised it. She'd spent ten years of her life working in A&E. It had always been her first choice. Always been her home. She'd never felt drawn to any other speciality and this was exactly why.

This was the moment that all department staff drew together. As she looked at the sea of faces—silently wishing there were a few more—she knew she could count on the colleagues around her. It was the same when any major casualties were expected. They were the biggest hospital in Dublin, with over six hundred beds. They always received the majority of casualties. They were always ready. And she was proud to be part of this team.

Iris Conway had done good. From the abandoned baby, to the adopted daughter of two parents who had rapidly became disinterested in her once they'd had a child of their own and then emigrated to Australia as soon as she'd gone to medical school, she only wished there was occasionally someone around to be proud of her and tell her so. That's why she relied on the team around her so much.

The doors burst open behind her, and the air rescue team ran in with their trolley, two of the A&E staff beside them. St Mary's had a helicopter landing pad on the roof, with direct access to a lift that brought them straight down to A&E.

The paramedic spoke quickly as the trolley rolled into Resus. The staff moved automatically, positioning themselves and quickly pulling the patient over. 'Owen Moore, twenty-seven. Part of the crew of the *McGonigal*. We think he was in the sea for approximately thirty minutes. Temperature currently twenty-eight degrees. Bradycardic, hypotensive. On oxygen, saturation ninety-two percent.'

Iris nodded. 'How long has he been out of the water?'

'Eight minutes.'

She held back the wow. These guys were real-life superheroes. 'You have more than one?'

'Second guy is coming in right behind us.' He paused and she knew there was something else.

'What?'

The doors crashed again, and she knew the second patient would be there in moments. He spoke into the radio pinned to his shoulder for a moment, then met her gaze. 'The winds have picked up again. Our second helicopter is having trouble landing.'

She gulped. Hoping her face wasn't showing the immediate thoughts in her head. As soon the first rescue craft had offloaded their patients, she knew it would have taken off again to leave room for its partner to land. These guys were experts.

The second trolley rolled into the room and she listened to the report. Almost identical to the first, only this guy was slightly older.

'Get the clothes off these guys. Both are right on the cusp between moderate and severe hypothermia. Recheck their temps. Cardiac monitoring is essential. Quick check for any other injuries and get me a blood glucose level and I need IV access and a set of bloods on both.'

She moved into position, next to the first patient, expertly sliding a Venflon into his shut-down peripheries. He was young. It was probably the only reason she'd managed to get venous access. She looked up to see Ryan, one of her other doctors, struggling to get access for the other patient. 'Need a hand?'

She could see the frustration on his face and knew he didn't want to give up. Sometimes with a hypothermic patient they had to put in a central line, or even use an infusion into the bone marrow. Taking over wouldn't help Ryan, but she'd do it if she had to. The needs of the patient always came first.

'I'm in,' he said after a few moments.

'Warming blankets,' she instructed, catching sight of the paramedic still at the door. She moved over and lowered her voice. 'Do you need someone to check you over?' Before she could stop herself, she reached over and touched his arm. It was icily cold, and that was through his jacket. 'Fergus?' Her shout echoed down the corridor, and the shaggy-haired nurse stuck his head out from behind a set of curtains. 'Take a look at our colleague for me,' she said, shaking her head as the paramedic tried to object. 'It will be a while before you can get back on duty,' she said quickly. 'I expect you want to hang around to make sure your other colleagues are fine anyway.'

She knew the words gave him the out. She'd been around these rescue guys for too many years. Looking after everyone else was always the priority over looking after themselves. He nodded as Fergus appeared and guided him away. He'd wanted to make sure the other helicopter landed safely and his fellow paramedic had delivered his own patients to the unit.

She moved, still assessing both patients. The

second guy, Euan, looked like he may have fractured a rib at some point. The radiographer appeared with the portable machine after a quick call.

The doors at the end of the corridor burst open again, and this time, one of her staff was on top of the trolley doing chest compressions. Relief firstly flooded over her as she realised the second helicopter must have landed safely, then disappeared rapidly at the acknowledgement of how sick the next patient was. 'Let's move these two guys to the bays at the side,' she said instantly, waving to the two patients currently in Resus. They would both still need constant monitoring, but at least they were certainly more stable than the patient on his way towards her.

Sean, one of their experienced anaesthetists, appeared. 'Call me your guardian angel. Just assessed the surgical patients,' he said quietly. 'Want me to hang around?'

'Absolutely,' she said instantly. Her brain wanted to question why he'd assessed the surgical patients instead of one of the actual surgeons, but there was no time for that.

The trolley swished in with the man being resuscitated. He was obviously older. 'Captain of the *McGonigal*,' said the ashen-faced paramedic. 'Was unconscious in the water by the time we winched him out. Had previously been conscious and told us we had to take all his crew first. Rob King. Fifty-seven.'

Her brain was trying hard to keep track of everything. 'Next guy's not quite as bad,' said the paramedic, as if he'd just read her thoughts.

Rena appeared in the doorway. 'New doc's just arrived. The replacement for Claire. He's looking after the two just moved out of Resus and seems to know his stuff. Ryan's breathing a sigh of relief.'

Iris gave a careful nod. Ryan was good, but only a year into the job. He didn't have enough experience yet, and she was glad the new doctor had arrived, because with patients like these, they really needed a doctor each.

She moved next to Sean, who had already expertly intubated Mr King and was attempting to get an IV in place, while the member of staff above kept chest compressions up. Iris wasn't in any way hierarchical. She wasn't going to tell Sean to let her take over, or move her staff member before she should. She seamlessly worked around them, placing the electrodes for the cardiac monitor around her colleagues' hands, taking a core temperature again and then a blood sugar reading. She wordlessly handed the warmed glucose IV line to Sean once he'd finished drawing off the bloods.

The fourth trolley rolled into place and Ryan came in on its heels. 'I'll take this one,' he said.

'What about the other two?'

'New guy's got them,' he said with an easy confidence that let her know they were in capable hands. She didn't even know the new guy's name.

She glanced quickly over at the fourth patient. Younger again, and he looked in a similar condition to the first two. Mr King was definitely the sickest. 'Lori,' she shouted to one of the other staff nurses. 'Come in and work with Ryan.'

Rena was bagging Mr King methodically. 'Wait!' Sean held his hand up to the nurse doing the compressions.

All eyes glanced at the monitor, and after a few moments of stuttering, a blip appeared. The nurse gave a sigh and jumped down from the trolley. 'Well done, Amy,' said Iris, tapping her staff member on the shoulder.

There was a shout from outside and Iris froze at the sound of the male voice.

It was almost like she'd jumped into the Irish Sea herself. Cold flooded through her veins and she was pretty sure her heart stopped.

Another voice joined in. Joan's. She was indignant and obviously giving someone a piece of her mind. Sean looked up. 'All yours,' he said, with a hint of a smile. 'I'll stay with Mr King.'

She was torn. Mr King was the sickest man here, and she was head of the department—she should be looking after him. But something was obviously awry in the next room, and as head of department, she should take control.

She knew exactly why her feet seemed to be sticking to the floor right now. But her brain hadn't really caught up with her body yet.

She could hear the ping, ping of the monitor in the cubicle next door. 'Stand clear,' came the steady male voice again, followed by the familiar sound of a shock being delivered.

'Move!' yelled Joan, and even though the words weren't aimed at Iris, they seemed to have the desired effect on her feet.

She took the few steps out of the resus room and into the bay next door.

A dark, slightly curled head was leaning over one of the patients from earlier who'd clearly gone into a cardiac arrest. The young medical student was practically pinned against the wall by Joan, an endotracheal tube clutched in one hand. Joan was barely five feet tall, and almost as wide, but she was a formidable force. 'You do not do anything in this department you are not qualified to do,' she hissed as she wordlessly handed a new sealed airway to the doctor beside her.

He glanced up, those familiar dark eyes locking on hers.

For a moment, the world froze. Lachlan Brodie. Her ex-husband. The man who'd stolen her heart years ago, and never given it back.

Lachlan looked just as shocked as she was, but in the blink of an eye, he was sliding the airway effortlessly into the patient's throat, moving to allow Joan to start bagging the patient. It was almost an echo of what was happening in the resus room right now.

She watched, still unable to move, as he turned his head to the monitor, checking the erratic beat of the man's heart. This wasn't uncommon in hypothermic patients. Episodes of ventricular fibrillation could occur in someone as their temperature rose.

'Temperature.' The words came out her mouth automatically, as the rules in these situations came back to her.

'Thirty,' came the curt reply. She grabbed adrenaline from the emergency cart and delivered it into the man's IV. 'Stand clear,' Lachlan repeated as he delivered a second shock.

A few seconds later, the heartbeat appeared again. But Iris didn't have time to breathe a sigh of relief. Because Lachlan straightened up and looked her in the eye. 'Tell me you're not in charge here?'

'Why?' was her stunned reply. Every tiny hair on the back of her neck stood indignantly on end.

'Because this is worst run department I've ever seen,' came the brutal, cutting response.

CHAPTER TWO

IT HAD ALL seemed too good to be true.

Which of course meant it was.

He'd barely registered with the agency when they'd contacted him with a job in Dublin, requiring an immediate start. It had taken two minutes of consideration—one, a quick look at the hospital, two, an even quicker search for the soonest flight.

Apparently one of their senior medics had let them down at the last minute leaving the perfect opportunity for someone with his experience to step in. The hospital manager hadn't cared he'd been out of A&E for the last few years spending time in general practice. His résumé beforehand was so good it practically sparkled and the manager had even offered to set up accommodation for him.

Three months in Ireland. It pretty much sounded like a dream come true. He'd never worked in Ireland before but had visited a few times and always wanted to see more of the place. The university hospital was the biggest in Dublin, with lots of attached specialities. It was set on one side of the city, so that if he chose to stay in either the city centre or the city suburbs, he would still have easy travel.

He'd asked the manager to find him a place in the suburbs or thereabouts, hoping to see a bit more of the countryside at some point, and the guy had sent him pictures of a gorgeous cottage that had made him instantly interested. A place with character. It's what he'd always wanted in a home.

The first minor hiccup had been when the plane had made three attempts to land at Dublin city airport due to the bad weather. The second hiccup had been when he'd put the cottage postcode into the hire car's navigation system and it had taken him on a tour of Ireland.

After many wrong turns, and asking a few people he passed, he finally made it to the cottage.

From that point, he'd felt as if everything would be plain sailing. The cottage had come stacked with a week's worth of groceries, wood in the wood burner, a local map showing where he could buy further supplies of both and a welcome note from the woman up the lane. She'd also left a tongue in cheek remark saying if he were a 'healthy' type and liked walking, he could take her dog with him. He'd smiled at that one. It had been years since Lachlan had been around dogs and he was more than happy to oblige.

The rain and winds had still been strong, and the sight of three waiting ambulances outside the A&E department let him know what to expect.

He'd had a quick introduction at HR, signed a few forms, shown proof of identity and his doctor registration and been supplied with his staff ID badge. It wasn't until he was walking down the stairs towards the A&E department that he realised he wasn't quite sure who to report to.

Five minutes later, he'd realised that was the last thing to worry about. The place was in pure and utter chaos. Every bay was full. Staff dashed from one place to another. Pagers sounded constantly, along with ringing phones that no one seemed to answer. He'd put his hand on the door of the staff room—heard someone sobbing inside—and realised it might not be the best introduction.

Then, as he'd headed towards the resus room—the most likely place to find the senior doctor on duty—he'd come across a nervous-looking doctor with two very sick patients.

Lachlan did what he would always do. Introduced himself, asked if he could help and assessed the situation. Both fishermen, both hypothermic and both pulled from the sea in the last hour. It didn't matter that it had been more than a few years since he'd looked after a properly hypothermic patient, he still knew all the basics. Raise core body temperature in a controlled manner to prevent any further problems.

The doctor's—Ryan—skills seemed sound. He just needed a bit of reassurance and some low-key instructions. Lachlan hadn't even had time to ask him who was in charge around here.

But there it was. That feeling. The one that he'd missed. The one that he'd craved. In barely a few seconds that frisson of excitement was already flooding his body. The rush of adrenaline, that instant switching on of his brain, acting on instinct, and being back at the heart of things.

The rush he felt working in A&E again was huge. He knew instantly this was the right move. Even if his first impressions were guarded, being put into a situation where he was immediately needed had kicked all his senses back into touch. He'd missed this. He'd missed this so much. And even though only a few milliseconds had passed he knew it had been the right decision to come back. He needed this. More than he'd ever known.

The last few years had been a strain. He'd moved to the English countryside with Lorraine, a fellow GP he'd cared about a lot. Lorraine had fallen ill, but what had seemed like a simple virus had the most horrendous impact on Lorraine. Viral cardiomyopathy, followed by rapid heart failure, and a position on the heart transplant list that had never been fulfilled. Of course, he'd stayed by her side all the way through. They might not have been in love in the traditional sense, but he'd felt genuine respect and affection for her. Lachlan had been the one holding her hand when she'd slipped away. One year on, he'd known the life of a rural GP wasn't for him long-term and he needed to get back to what he loved. This. Emergency medicine.

He could see another two emergencies being rushed in, and immediately realised one was being resuscitated. Whoever was in charge was clearly where they needed to be. When Ryan had disappeared a few moments later, he'd appreciated it was likely a time of all hands on deck.

The curtain between the two cubicles was half pulled, and as soon the monitor started pinging, Lachlan strode around to pull it back properly so he could observe both patients clearly.

All his senses went on alert at the view on the monitor. He reached instantly for the defib, slapping two pads on the patient's chest. 'Stand clear,' he said loudly, checking, before delivering a shock.

He'd barely had time to blink before he witnessed a young man being hauled away from the patient by one of the fiercest nurses he'd ever seen. 'What's going on?'

The nurse glared at him. 'Who are you?'

'Lachlan Brodie, new A&E consultant.' He changed position, focusing his attention on the patient in front of him who'd gone into ventricular fibrillation. His heart wasn't beating properly and without intervention he could die.

'Joan,' came the brisk reply. She stopped pinning the young man to the wall and snatched what he now realised was an endotracheal tube from his hand. 'Our med student keeps trying to do a procedure he isn't trained for.'

She literally bumped the student out of the way with her large hips.

Lachlan kept entirely calm, even though he could feel the rage building inside. Where was all the qualified staff? Who was looking after all these patients? And why was a student left unsupervised?

He spoke smoothly as he assessed the young man in front of him and scanned his chart in a few seconds. 'Well, there are no breath sounds. We need to maintain an airway here.' He reached his hand out to the nearby emergency trolley but before he could pull anything, Joan wordlessly handed him a new sealed airway, tilting the patient's head back. 'You can watch,' he said to the student at the side. 'We start with a standard airway—not an endotracheal tube straight away. And we continually assess our patient.'

He'd barely slid the airway into place before the nurse had deftly attached the oxygen supply to the bag and mask and handed it over. Not a word had been said. She clearly knew what she was doing.

But that was when it all went wrong. That was when the ground seemed to slide out from under his feet.

It was slow motion. The smell first. That familiar perfume he'd only ever known one person to wear and it sent prickles across his skin. The sense of someone at the foot of the trolley. That all-knowing feeling that someone was watching. For the briefest second he glanced upwards. No. No. It couldn't be Iris. It was just his mind playing tricks on him.

'Temperature?' came the oh-so-familiar voice.

He answered on automatic pilot. 'Thirty.' He

knew exactly why she was asking as he moved again and nodded to Joan to start bagging the patient. He needed to deliver another shock. The person—who he really, really hoped was a figment of his imagination—grabbed some adrenaline from the cart. Patients with a temperature under thirty weren't allowed adrenaline. This guy had made it by the skin of his teeth.

'Clear,' he instructed again, wondering if he was actually still on the plane circling above Dublin and he'd fallen asleep, and this was all just some bizarre kind of nightmare.

He delivered the shock and waited a few seconds, eyes on the monitor. It gave a blip, then a reassuring other blip, followed by something that started to resemble a reasonable heart rate.

Lachlan breathed, and realised his mistake, as he got a complete intake of her perfume again, and all the sensations that triggered in his body. All the memories that related to that smell.

Eight years. That's how long it was since he'd seen Iris Conway, his ex-wife. And right now, eight years didn't seem long enough.

He'd had—what, two minutes of bliss to relish being back in the job? And now, he was tumbling head over heels into some weird parallel universe.

The girl he'd married when they were twenty-three after only knowing her a few, passionate months, vowing never to regret it. Three years later they'd both regretted it and she'd completely and utterly broken his heart.

They'd parted ways, severing any mutual friendships between them. He didn't need or want to know where she was in the world, or what she was doing. He'd always wanted her to have a good and happy life, but his battered and bruised heart didn't feel the need to see it or hear about it.

Lachlan knew he was unprepared for this reunion. He'd always suspected that Iris would continue in the profession they'd both loved. But the world was a big place and he'd just never expected to run into her again.

He couldn't help all the sensations that bubbled up inside him. He couldn't stop the instant annoyance and blame that spilled over. 'Tell me you're not in charge here?'

He knew his tone spoke a thousand other words. Dripping with sarcasm and holding an edge of contempt. He sensed immediately the staff around him tensing as he continued to work on his patient. Of course it was a mistake—to be the new guy and speak to an existing physician like that. But no one else got it. No one else knew their history. The angry

words. The broken hearts. The huge regrets
that had bubbled between them. How on earth
could they?

'Why?' Iris's response was everything. Indignant. Defensive. And hurt.

And again, he couldn't stop himself. 'Because this is worst run department I've ever
seen.'

He could hear the intake of breath all around
him. How to win friends and influence people
at a brand-new place of work. *First impressions count.*

But somehow, the normally professional,
easy-going life that Lachlan usually inhabited
had just plummeted off a cliff edge.

For a second he locked eyes with his wife.
Ex-wife, he reminded himself. Her blonde hair
was high in a ponytail and her pale blue eyes
raged at his. She was a bit thinner than the last
time he'd seen her. It gave her face a pinched
edge that didn't suit Iris and gave the overall
impression of stress. He'd no idea what had
happened in her life since they'd parted company—just like she'd no idea what had happened in his. Maybe it showed in his face too?
He'd never really considered it before now.

Her voice had a tiny hint of a tremble, and he
wondered if her colleagues noted it the same
way that he did. 'Not the time, Dr Brodie. Treat

your patients, and we will take this up later. In private.' The words held a special emphasis that almost sounded like a threat. She turned and strode away.

Iris was mad. Lachlan had seen Iris mad in many guises in the past. But today he didn't feel sad about it. Didn't feel like he wanted to run after her and force her into a discussion she didn't want anyway.

Darn it. He should have researched this job better. He should have looked up every doctor that worked here. In his haste to get away from his previous job and memories of Lorraine, he'd taken the first thing available. And if something seemed too good to be true—it generally was. Lachlan had been around the block a few times, he knew this. He couldn't believe he'd allowed himself to be caught out like this.

He blinked and was instantly swamped by the cold feeling around him. He glanced at the patient monitor and barked out a few other instructions. Joan, the nurse, gave him a look that told him exactly where he stood with the rest of the staff. Yep, it seemed whilst he'd thought he was falling off a cliff edge when he glimpsed Iris, the words that he'd spoken to her had dropped him into a sea as icy as the one these fishermen had just been pulled from. Perfect.

Joan followed his instructions as he contin-

ued to treat the two young men. The medical
student clearly didn't know where to look, so
Lachlan just spoke out loud, telling him everything he was doing, and the reasons behind it.
He dropped in a few questions, to make sure
the student understood and was paying attention.

After around half an hour, Lachlan felt comfortable with the condition of both men. He
could still hear murmuring from the resus room
next door. His eyes met Joan's steely grey gaze.
'Is assistance needed next door?'

'Dr Conway has everything under control,'
she snapped back. She hadn't moved from his
side, and unless she possessed telepathic capa-
bilities she couldn't possibly know that.

He stopped himself from pointing out the
fact and gave her a half-smile. 'Then perhaps
you want to check on your colleague in the staff
room. They seemed pretty upset.'

She blinked, clearly surprised that he knew
that. But her response was just as quick. 'Fergus is already on that.' She picked up some
empty packaging and clinical waste. 'Just like
Dr Conway instructed,' she added over her
shoulder as she headed to get rid of the waste.

Lachlan took a few moments. He didn't really need to stand over these patients. But he
wasn't leaving them unsupervised. The place

was still busy. He was sure there were more patients he could be seeing right now, but he'd clearly sealed his popularity around here.

He turned to the medical student. 'Okay, let's start from scratch. Hypothermic patient, brought in like this.' He handed over the chart the paramedic had brought with him. 'Talk me through the complete treatment plan, and the rationale behind it.'

It took a while, and Lachlan knew it was because the student was nervous. Another doctor appeared and stuck out his hand. 'Ajat,' he said. 'I'm from ITU. I heard these two were coming up to our step-down beds for close observation for a few hours.'

Lachlan gave a nod. It made sense. They weren't ventilated, but could still deteriorate at a moment's notice. He gave a handover for both patients, signed off on the drugs given and stood back as they were both transferred somewhere upstairs. At some point, he would have to take a look around this state-of-the-art hospital.

He'd barely moved out of the cubicles and walked over to the whiteboard to see where else he could be of help before he heard a voice at his shoulder. 'Staff room. Now.'

Iris was standing at his right shoulder. He hadn't even heard her approach.

She didn't wait, just strode off in front of him, knocking the door of the staff room with her hip and leaving it swinging behind her.

Lachlan was almost tempted to smile. It had been a long time since he'd seen an Iris work-related rage.

The staff room was empty, and he realised instantly that she'd known this before bringing him here.

She walked over and flicked the switch on a kettle, before turning around, arms folded across her chest. 'Don't you dare criticise my department. Who do you think you are, walking in here, and talking to me like that in front of my staff?'

The part of his brain that was rational had a momentary explosion. What was it about Iris that made all his functioning parts lose the ability to communicate with one another?

'You're right, I'm sorry. Not the best first impression to make, I admit. But I walked into a department that was clearly in chaos. Every bay full. A doctor who looked out of his depth. A medical student who wanted to tube someone at the first blink of a cardiac arrest. A nurse who had to get him under control. Another staff member weeping. And a department that doesn't have a hope of meeting its target for waiting times—and that's before I've even looked in the waiting room.'

He saw the muscles tense at the bottom of her throat and around her shoulders. 'I'm four doctors down. My most experienced staff aren't here today, and some people have had to step up. You know how that works—it happens in every A&E department. The storm has caused an unexpected surge in cases. The wards are full, we have no beds. St Mary's is currently on a purple alert—as are the other emergency receiving units throughout Dublin. We can't get people discharged home, because ambulance services are struggling.' She licked her lips. He knew she was angry, but the expression on her face was bland, as if she were just reiterating the facts to some nameless enquirer.

'All my bays are full, because the other specialities are struggling to get down and assess their patients. My waiting room is full too, but all patients have been triaged and at least they're safe from the storm whilst they're in my waiting room. I care not a jot about meeting waiting times in a situation like this. I only care about keeping patients safe.'

He broke in before she could continue. 'So, that's why you left a clearly inexperienced doctor and a random unsupervised medical student on the loose?'

She held up her hand as a clear sign he should stop talking *right now*. 'Ryan is not inexperienced. He's perfectly capable. He's been here a year and is still building his confidence. He just hasn't dealt with a half-drowned, hypothermic fisherman before. It's not an everyday occurrence and hardly a crime.'

Okay, Lachlan's insides might have cringed a little. He'd quickly realised that Ryan wasn't incapable and just needed a few prompts.

She kept going. 'Our medical student is brand new. I haven't had time to assess him yet because I've been treating patients. However, Joan—and I know you've met her—is one of my best nurses. She's all over him, and I suspect that's exactly what he needs.'

'What he needs is adequate supervision and a proper teaching environment.'

'Both of which he'll get. Here, under my watch. Heaven help a member of staff take two minutes to wash their hands between patients, Lachlan.'

Lachlan. The way she said his name sparked a million memories. Half of them good. Half of them not so good. But the weirdest thing was, even though his stomach twisted painfully inside, it was the good pictures that flashed into his head. Iris, laughing in her gorgeous wedding gown, holding her yellow flowers next to her face. Iris, leaning forward to kiss his cheek. Iris, sighing happily in the morning, and the glint in her eye as she tried to convince him that it was his turn to make breakfast, knowing full well it was hers. Iris and him, snuggled on their lumpy sofa dreaming about having a family of their own and whether they would have boys that looked like Lachlan, or girls that looked like Iris.

All of those memories rushing out of nowhere and filling his brain in less than a second. It had been a long time since he'd allowed himself time and space to think about Iris.

He straightened his spine and tried to bring himself back to the here and now.

'Criticising your department wasn't a great start. But you still have staff running around like headless chickens and far too many patients waiting to be assessed.' He looked around the empty room. 'And what does it say about a department if you have a member of staff in here, crying?'

Her lips tightened. 'It says we have a place where staff can come and take five minutes out their day when they're feeling overwhelmed and need a little space.'

'It also makes me question if they are getting adequate support from the people around them.' It was a really low blow and he knew that. But the person he usually was seemed to have been left outside in the storm somewhere.

She turned her back to him and took out a mug—two mugs—filling them with a heap of coffee and pouring boiling water into both.

'This won't work,' she said as she handed him a cup.

He didn't answer, not knowing quite how to respond, but completely agreeing.

'It's not a good idea for us to work together. I can't have you disrupting my department like this.'

He let out a wry laugh. '*I'm* disrupting your department?'

For the first time, the rigid expression on her face disappeared and her shoulders seemed to sag a little.

Her eyes focused elsewhere. 'But I've been let down at short notice. So, you can't go until someone fills your place.'

The cottage sprang into his mind. He'd barely even had a chance to see the place and had already signed a three-month lease. He didn't want to walk out on his elderly neighbour and leave her in the lurch.

'I have dog walking responsibilities,' he said with a hint of humour in his voice.

'What?' Iris looked stunned. Whatever she'd expected him to say, it hadn't been that.

He nodded and sipped the coffee. Black, with nothing. Just like how she took hers. Years of working in A&E departments had taught them both that any milk that hadn't been used yet was likely out of date. They'd learned to drink coffee with no embellishments. She'd remembered. She'd remembered how he took his coffee.

Something speared through him. He'd come here to rediscover his love for work. His love for life.

The irony of coming across the love of his life in that process wasn't lost on him. But Iris wasn't his reason for being here.

'If I'd known you were here, I wouldn't have come,' he admitted.

For the briefest second she looked hurt, and then she looked relieved. He didn't even know what that meant.

'Why did you come?' This time the question was in a softer voice. Iris was curious. Curious about him.

More irony. Lachlan had always been certain that as much as he'd never really wanted to know about how Iris was getting on in life, the feeling had been mutual. They'd parted ways, and never expected them to cross again.

He didn't owe her anything. And she didn't owe him anything either.

He ran a hand through his hair. 'I've been out of A&E for a few years. Tried something different, my circumstances changed, and I decided to come back.' He paused for a moment, wishing he hadn't mentioned his circumstances. He didn't want to answer any real questions about his life since they split up—just the most generic things. 'I guess I'm just trying to reignite the fire for my work that I used to have.'

There. It was out in the open. But he couldn't pretend that the tiny flare he'd felt less than an hour ago hadn't happened.

To her credit, Iris let the words sit for a few moments. 'I need someone with experience,' she said slowly. 'And no matter what you've done for the last few years—unless it was time in prison—I know how good an A&E doctor you are.' Her eyes were on his. He saw the briefest hesitation.

He gave a half-smile. 'I can assure you I wasn't in prison.' He didn't offer any more.

She licked her lips and nodded again cautiously. He could see the doubts written all over her face. He knew she was weighing things up in her head.

'This is my department. And I can put the needs of my department before my own feelings.'

'Well, that sounds reassuring.' He shook his

head, already knowing where this was going. If he were in Iris's position, would he be saying the same words?

'I need an experienced A&E doctor,' she said steadily. 'One whose work I can trust.'

He leaned back against the worktop in the staff room. 'I'm not too sure I've created the best first impression with your staff. I fear they might want to club me to death in some cubicle.'

The edges of her lips hinted upwards. 'My staff are fiercely loyal. Some of them have been here longer than I have. If you cause trouble, or say anything about me, prepare to be thrown into the Irish Sea.'

He shuddered. 'After the state of those men today? Not likely.'

'I may also ask you to supervise the medical students.'

'It's a punishment, isn't it?'

This time she did smile and shake her head. 'Not at all. I just know that after our initial encounter, you still spent some time teaching Mr Over-Enthusiastic some of things that I would expect from a mentor working in a university hospital.' But there was a hint of humour on her face. 'And yes, it's your punishment for your initial comment. You are now officially in charge of the students.'

Lachlan stayed silent for a few minutes, trying to sort all this out in his head. He'd landed in a beautiful country, lucked out with accommodation and scored a job in a hospital that would look good on his CV. But could he and his ex-wife really work together?

'What will you tell your staff about me?'

She swallowed. 'The truth. I'll tell them you're my ex-husband. They know I was married before, but I've never given them details.' A tiny flare of hurt crossed her eyes and he looked away. 'It's been eight years. I'll tell them I know you're a good doctor. You came here at short notice to fill a gap that badly needed filling, and neither of us knew about the other.'

She nodded her head as if the idea was cementing in her head. 'Anything else would be complicated. I don't lie to my staff. They'll know that we'll be a bit awkward around each other. They might ask a few questions—but I'd be obliged if our private life could remain private.'

He glanced at her hand. It suddenly occurred to him that yes, it had been eight years. He knew exactly what had happened to him in those eight years, but he'd no idea what had happened to her. She could have happily moved on and be married with three kids right now. His presence might ruffle other feathers in the hospital—what if her husband worked here like she did? He didn't want that. He didn't want his presence to affect anyone else.

'Apart from you and me, will this arrangement cause problems for anyone else?'

It was if she had a moment of fleeting panic. 'What do you mean?'

'I mean, are you married? Do you have a fiancé, or boyfriend, in the hospital or local area that will object to us working together? I don't want to cause any problems. I genuinely had no idea you were here.'

He felt as if he had to say it out loud. Deep down, he had wanted Iris to be happy, and if she was, his being here might impact on that.

'There's no husband,' she said with a nervous laugh. 'No fiancé, no boyfriend. Not right now.' She held out her arms. 'Work keeps me busy, as you can see.'

He gave a slow nod. 'So, we can do this? We can make this work?'

'Honestly, I have no idea. But we're adults. We should at least try.'

Those blue eyes held his gaze for the briefest of seconds before she threw her coffee down the sink and rinsed her mug. 'Now, come on. I have about ten patients I want you to see.'

She was back to business. Back to being head

of a department. And that felt easier. Simpler for them both.

So, he followed her lead. Dumped his coffee, washed his mug and followed her back outside into the chaos.

CHAPTER THREE

IT WAS STILL THERE. That instant recognition. That feeling that had shot up her spine at first sight of him. Now, instead of a quick shock, it was remaining a steady tingle, a hum, sending all of her other senses into overdrive.

She'd given her staff the briefest explanation that Lachlan was her ex-husband, and that they'd both been shocked by seeing each other after eight years. Both Joan and Rena had raised their eyebrows. Neither was happy with his initial words about their department and boss, and both had made their feelings known.

But since another doctor had just phoned in sick, Iris had made it clear that he had apologised to her, and the department's priority was to have a doctor with the skills they needed. She'd assured them that Lachlan was a good doctor, good with patients and good with students. It only took a few days for them and the surrounding staff to see that for themselves.

A paediatric emergency, two road traffic accidents and quick recognition of a case of malaria—something they rarely saw in Dublin—seemed to seal Lachlan's abilities in their minds.

But none of it did anything to help Iris's peace of mind.

Things would be much simpler if Lachlan wasn't here. His quiet chat with older patients, his reassurance to anxious parents and his empathetic delivery of bad news to relatives were all sparking memories that sat uncomfortably with her.

He'd always been a good doctor. He'd also been a good husband. Until other issues had driven them apart. They'd both been keen to have a family. Lachlan, as an only child himself with elderly parents, had wanted a large family of his own. Iris had always been honest about being adopted, but she hadn't told him anything of the really tough stuff about her life. She'd been bitterly hurt when her adoptive parents had given birth to their own child and virtually ignored her. She knew she hadn't helped matters by playing up and attention seeking, which had only made their relationship worse. She'd brushed off Lachlan's questions, saying she wasn't that close to her family, and that they'd emigrated to Australia when she started university. Those parts had been entirely true. It was hard to tell the man who had turned her world upside down and captured her heart so quickly that her family had never loved her the way he had. Lachlan was everything to her, and having a family together had seemed like the best idea in the world. Planning their family had started out being fun, and had then turned into a more serious, concerted effort to conceive.

Iris knew that she'd become a little obsessed. Everyone around her seemed to be falling pregnant—everyone but her. After a year she'd wanted to do tests. Lachlan hadn't been so keen, telling her to wait another year and give it some time. She knew that was the normal advice to give in this situation. But this wasn't normal. This was about *them*.

She'd badgered and badgered, and they'd finally both undergone tests. All of which had shown there was nothing wrong—with either of them.

After private consultations, more tests, a few rounds of intrauterine insemination, followed by unsuccessful in vitro fertilisation, their lack of success had left them both ragged and upset. There was no clinical reason for them not to be pregnant. Nothing scientific. Apparently, they just weren't a good 'match.'

It was a useless explanation that left frustration and resentment building in them both.

After a while Lachlan had been keen to pursue other options—adoption mainly. But Iris couldn't get there. Every time she looked at the man she loved with her whole heart, she felt as if she'd failed him, and he in turn had failed her.

She'd refused counselling, probably because she'd not been ready to accept that she needed it.

Her mood had dipped lower and lower. When Lachlan had suggested she seek other help, she'd been furious. She knew she hadn't coped well. She knew that she'd fixated on being pregnant, and her whole body had been stressed beyond belief. But none of that helped. And none of that made her want to repair the relationship with her husband that was rapidly deteriorating.

So, they'd split up. Both broken-hearted. Divorced, and walked away to make a fresh start.

She'd never imagined their paths would cross again.

Because she'd never imagined what she'd need to tell him if they did.

Iris had healed—eventually. After a few half-hearted relationships that fizzled out quickly, she'd spent some time on her own, found an amazing counsellor and accepted her life as it was, taking pleasure in her job, her achievements and her friendships.

Her counsellor had spent hours with her,

picking apart her own feelings of rejection by her adoptive parents, the fears and resentments she'd had when her husband had suggested they go down the route of adoption and the deep, deep horror that she might ever act towards any child she adopted the same way her parents had.

It had taken her a long time to accept that the whole experience of not being able to conceive and the subsequent breakdown of her marriage had left her with unrecognised, and untreated, depression. Once she'd acknowledged that, her path to acceptance that she was not the same as her parents, had been a less steep hill to climb.

So, when she'd made the decision to look at adoption as a single mother, she'd felt ready to take that step. She'd gone through all the assessment processes and finally been approved. And she'd done all that here, in Dublin, the place she'd come to with her broken heart, to heal and repair herself.

She had close friends outside the hospital who knew her whole story. But she'd always been a little more protective about what she shared with her colleagues at work. They knew she had a daughter. They knew her daughter was adopted. Most of them had met Holly at some point or another. But they didn't know that her husband had once asked her to consider adoption. To think about expanding their family in a way that didn't put her body under constant pressure. To take a break from all the drugs, and the counting days, the incessant calendar watching.

Or to maybe realise that being a family of two was more than enough.

It had been her that had said no. It had been her that had said it wasn't enough for her. It had been her that had refused to take a break, or step away and truly consider adoption as a way forward for them. She just couldn't bring herself to dig deep and tell Lachlan about her own true experience of adoption. She'd spent so much of her life feeling unloved and unwanted that being unable to manage the supposedly simple step of becoming pregnant and giving her husband the big family he'd so freely told her he wanted had made her feel totally useless and unworthy again. All things she just couldn't vocalise to him, too ashamed to admit what she perceived as her failings.

So when adoption had been mentioned, she'd point-blank refused. Wouldn't even properly consider it. And he'd seemed to accept her decision easily, which left her feeling as if it wasn't an option he'd really wanted to pursue anyhow. So, in a way, she'd stolen that option from them both—then stolen it back, entirely for herself.

Now, eight years on, she knew exactly why her stomach turned in knots at the thought of someone revealing to Lachlan that she'd adopted a child.

She couldn't specifically ask her staff not to mention Holly. That was wrong. Holly was the brightest part of her life. But she could ask her staff in a more general way not to mention her personal life to Lachlan. And she did. In the most low-key way possible. 'Lachlan and I used to be married, so you know things might be a little awkward for a while,' were the words she'd used casually. 'He's a great doctor, and a great person, and I want you all to get to know him. So, to keep things simple for us all, it's probably best if you keep things professional and don't talk about us personally around each other.'

She'd noticed the quick exchange of glances. But her staff had nodded as if it were no big deal.

But that hadn't helped the constant churning of her stomach ever since. He was only here on a temporary contract. If he stayed any longer than the three months he'd signed up for, she would tell him. Of course she would—when the time was right. And that was what she kept telling herself.

Dublin was an interesting city. There were a whole load of distillery and whisky tours to be done. Museums were next on the list, with one even at a cemetery. But what Lachlan hadn't counted on was the ever-present coach tours on every country road.

Staying slightly outside the city had seemed like a good idea. He'd spent many a good hour tramping across the countryside with Scout, the fierce terrier belonging to Maeve at the top of the lane. A few quick conversations had made him realise that Maeve's arthritis had slowed her physical fitness, so when Lachlan's phone had rung at nine o'clock one night, he'd assumed that Maeve was checking to see if he could take Scout out the next day.

'Lachlan?' The normally cheery voice sounded distinctly trembly.

'Is something wrong?' He sat up straight away.

'I've had a bit of tumble. I hate to do this, but I can't quite get up. Could you come and help me.'

Lachlan's feet were already in his boots. He kept his phone pressed to his ear as he opened his door and started half running, half striding down the lane. 'Is your door open, Maeve?'

'Of course it's open. Why would I lock it?'

Lachlan shook his head, keeping the whole host of responses he could give a back seat, trying not to think about the fact he'd just done exactly the same thing.

'I'm nearly there. Hold on. Don't try and move. I'll check you over first, before we try and get you up.' He could hear a quiet yap from Scout. 'Is Scout okay?'

Maeve gave a nervous laugh. 'I think he knows something is wrong. He keeps coming over and looking at me.'

Lachlan reached the blue door and gave a few knocks before he entered. Scout almost pounced on him, appearing like a speeding bullet from the back of cottage, giving a few growls, a few barks and then winding between his legs. Lachlan bent down and rubbed his head. 'Don't worry, old guy. I'll sort her out,' he said softly.

'Maeve, I'm here. Let's see you.' Maeve's cottage was similar to his own; it only took a few long strides to go between the rooms. Maeve was lying on the carpet in the main sitting room, in an awkward position between the chair and coffee table.

'What do you mean let's see you?' she said scoldingly. 'What kind of sight is this to see?'

Lachlan knelt down the floor next to her, pushing the heavy coffee table out of the way to get more room. 'Sorry, it's an expression of my gran's.'

Maeve's face was much paler than usual and the smile on her face was clearly forced. 'I'm just a silly old fool. I can't get my legs under me to get back up.'

Alarm bells started going off in his head. 'How did you feel before you fell? Were you light-headed, dizzy?'

She wrinkled her brow. 'I'm not sure.' She winced as she tried to move.

Lachlan moved closer, pulling a cushion from the sofa. 'I'm going to put this under your head, lie back for a moment.'

He gave Maeve a quick check. At this age, it could be anything. A stroke, TIA, hypotension. Bones were so fragile at this age—any fall could cause a multitude of fractures. As he had no pen torch, he pulled out his phone to check her pupils, then gave her a quick pat down, noting she winced as he touched her ribs.

'Has this happened before?' Scout was sniffing around them both, obviously concerned.

Maeve gave a shrug, her breathing a little ragged. 'Once or twice. Only when I get up too quickly.'

'Did you get checked over?'

She waved one hand. 'I was fine.'

'But you're not fine. I'm going to take you to my workplace and give you a check over. I suspect you might have fractured a rib, but I want to check a few other things too.'

'Can't you just help me up? I'll be fine.'

'I wouldn't be a very good doctor if I just helped you up into a chair, and left it to happen again, would I?'

She sighed and rolled her eyes.

'Okay, I'm sure your legs and arms are fine, so let me take your weight and sit you in the chair. Then, I'm going to get my car, and take you for a check at the hospital.'

He could have called an ambulance—and if he'd thought for a second Maeve had broken her hip or any other leg bones, he would have left her on the floor until he had help to assist him. He was also sure she hadn't broken her shoulder and could therefore assist her up without doing any damage.

It only took a few moments to help her up onto the nearest armchair, and make sure she was safe, before he ran back down the lane to pick up his car. He brought it right up to Maeve's front door—much to Scout's indignation—and helped her out into the front passenger seat. His arm was gripped firmly around her waist and he watched with interest when he first helped her upright, saying nothing but clocking her symptoms.

The journey to the hospital was swift—the

roads were quieter at this time in Dublin—and he pulled up directly into an empty ambulance bay. Ray, one of the porters, was out straight away, ready to shout at the impromptu parking, but clocked quickly it was Lachlan. 'What do you need?'

'Do you have a wheelchair?'

With a nod, Ray came up alongside and they both helped Maeve into the wheelchair. 'Do you want me to take her inside, or do you want me to move your car?'

It was an easy decision. He handed his car keys over to Ray. 'Much appreciated.'

'No bother, Doc.'

He was grateful. After an initial frosty start, the staff had started to become less wary of him. He'd noticed that none of them mentioned Iris around him—except in relation to patients—and that was fine. The uneasy truce between them still caused mixed emotions. This wasn't the fresh start he'd wanted.

If he walked around the department when Iris was on shift he could smell traces of her perfume. She'd worn it for years, a light floral scent that was more or less her signature. He would hear her laugh when talking to other people, and it seemed to skitter across his skin in a way he didn't want to admit.

His brain was itching to know about the last

eight years—but of course he couldn't ask. He deliberately hadn't told anyone about himself. There had been a few casual conversations with physicians from other departments where he'd mentioned working as a GP for the last few years. There had also been a few conversations with the cardiology team around patients that had presented in A&E with partly suspicious symptoms. Fortunately, on two occasions his instincts had been correct, and he'd been complimented on his good catches, leading to earlier treatment for those patients.

He knew he was influenced by his time with Lorraine. It was only natural, and had given him some insights on unusual cardiac symptoms control that could easily be missed.

As he wheeled Maeve straight through to the bays, he picked up a portable tablet to enter her details. Rena appeared at her side. 'You working tonight, Lachlan?'

He smiled and glanced down at his jeans, dirty trainers and navy walking jacket. 'Not really, but looks like it. This is my neighbour, Maeve. She's had a fall and might have fractured a rib. I want to get her checked over and investigate a few things about her fall.'

Rena flashed a smile at Maeve, and from her glance at him he knew she could read between the lines. 'Let me give you a hand.'

He nodded gratefully and they helped Maeve onto a trolley. Rena pulled the curtains, took some quick details and ordered an X-ray whilst Lachlan checked and recorded Maeve's obs. 'Sitting and standing BP?' she asked, and Lachlan nodded.

Lachlan was aware that Rena still gave him the odd cautious glance, but she was a clear winner with the patients and he was grateful for her assistance. Ray appeared again to take Maeve for her X-ray and Rena gave him a few words of instructions for the technicians in the X-ray department.

Lachlan took the opportunity to walk along to the nurses' station to see how the night was going. Everyone on the whiteboard was assigned to a doctor and things seemed remarkably calm. Iris looked up in surprise. She was wearing a pair of black trousers and a short-sleeved yellow shirt. 'You look like a big sunflower.' He smiled as he sagged into the chair next to her.

'What on earth are you doing here?' she said, before glancing down at her shirt. 'And thanks, yellow is my new favourite colour, and pay attention, there are daises printed on this shirt. I did have on a green top, but you know how things are in A&E.'

He pulled a face. 'Vomit or blood?'

She shook her head. 'Coffee, actually.'

'Still clumsy?'

The words came out automatically without much thought. Their gazes connected as a million memories flashed by in his head. Iris dropping their toast, butter side down, on the kitchen floor every other morning. Cups of tea and coffee being knocked or spilled constantly throughout the household. Her occasional trait of walking into half-shut doors or doorframes because she'd been distracted by either her phone or a book—or just too busy talking in general.

Her mouth turned upwards in a private smile and her words were quiet. 'Eternally clumsy,' she replied.

'Are we taking bets on that shirt, then?' He leaned back in his chair and clasped his hands. 'It's too pale for A&E. I give you less than fifteen minutes.'

She sighed and nodded in agreement. 'I should have put on a scrub top. But I'm tired of always wearing scrubs. This was in my locker and just seemed to call to me.'

Lachlan gestured to outside. 'Because it suits the weather?'

Iris groaned and put her head on the desk. 'I can't believe it's still so bad. That's been, what, two weeks?'

He grinned. 'I tell you, none of the travel ad-verts for Ireland show weather like this—it's all sunshine, cloudless skies and bright green hills.'

She turned her head sideways and narrowed her gaze. 'Hey, maybe it's your fault. Maybe you brought this weather with you?'

This is what it used to be like between them. Easy. Relaxed. Joking, most of the time. Until it all changed. 'Of course I did,' he said. 'I delib-erately brought the bad weather with me. Made my flight circle three times before I landed, overturned those boats in the Irish Sea and con-tinually battered my little cottage with wind and rain so the windows rattle.'

She tilted her head at him. 'You're staying in a cottage?'

'Yep, just on the outskirts of the city, a bit further out.'

She wrinkled her nose. 'Did you want to be outside the city?'

He gave a quiet shrug, wondering how much to reveal. 'I'm in Dalkey.'

Her eyes almost boggled. 'That's the Hol-lywood hills of Dublin; it must be costing you a fortune. How on earth can you afford that? You do know several celebrities live there, don't you?' He watched as she realised what she had said and put a hand to her mouth. 'Sorry, that didn't come out quite right.'

He gave a slow nod. 'It took me a few days to catch on. Maeve—the lady I've brought in—stays just up the lane. She owns both cottages. They've been in her family for decades and she started renting one out a few years ago to the hospital for visiting nurses or doctors for a small fee. Apparently, she prefers us to the "ridiculous holiday crowd."' He gave a small laugh. 'Wait till you meet her. She does know she could sell both and make a fortune, or renovate and extend them with glass and steel, but she isn't the slightest bit interested.' He gave Iris a knowing smile. In the midst of a generally busy department, it was rare to get some uninterrupted moments. This was really the first time they'd sat and chatted. He'd missed her, he realised. He'd missed her more than he ever wanted to admit. A tiny bit of blonde hair had escaped her ponytail and his fingers itched to tuck it behind her ear.

He'd shut this whole part of his brain off. The Iris part. Because remembering had just been too painful. But now he had no choice but to remember, as Iris was continually in his sights.

'So, what's the cottage like?' She seemed genuinely interested. 'You always wanted something old.'

It appeared that Iris remembered just as much as he did. 'Lots of character. Small but not too small. There's two bedrooms, a main sitting room that the front door opens straight into. A kitchen with the real-life genuine stove, and one bathroom with rattling pipes.' He gave a laugh. 'There's a wood burner installed that gives off a surprising amount of heat, and the place has a new roof, which is just as well.'

'Because?'

'Because a huge amount of heat must stream out the old windows. I'm tempted to find a silicon gun and seal some of the gaps, but I guess there must be some kind of order on the house as a listed building.'

Iris leaned her chin on her hands, her eyes straight on him. 'But think of all the cottages around there that have been renovated and look nothing like the original.'

He shrugged. 'It's not mine, but I'm already starting to love it.'

She made a small clicking sound with her tongue and sat back in her chair folding her arms. 'But you can't *really* love it.'

It was the way she'd said those words. The joke they'd always held between them about their ideal house and what it would have.

He nodded in agreement. 'You're right. There's no room for a library.'

Iris shifted in her seat and pulled a face. 'I hate to tell you this…'

She let her voice trail off.

'You do not?' His voice was indignant.

She gave a not-so-sorry shoulder shrug as her eyes gleamed. 'I do so.'

'You have a library, in your house? Where do you stay?'

He watched something flit across her eyes. She obviously felt the same way he did, reluctant to give too much away. But she'd brought it up. She couldn't back down now. 'I stay in Portobello, in a red brick period terraced house.'

He rolled his eyes. 'Trendy. And as the saying goes, how do you afford that?'

Even though he'd only been there a few weeks, Lachlan had still managed to take a walk around Portobello. The houses were on the pricier side, the area was surrounded with lots of nice cafés, bars and restaurants, and was a short walk into the city centre.

Iris's face fell for a moment. 'Aunt Lucy died.'

His reaction was immediate and he couldn't help himself. He reached out and put his hand over hers. 'I'm so sorry, I had no idea.'

Iris's aunt Lucy had been an elderly spinster, absolutely adorable, with a million stories, sparkling wit and a big heart. She was the only member of Iris's family that he'd met; Lachlan had adored her, and his heart gave a sad lurch to hear she was gone.

But something else came over him immediately. Skin. It was the first time he'd touched Iris's skin in for ever… And although the gesture had been purely for comfort, there was a whole host of sparks shooting up his arm right now. Sparks that were entirely inappropriate, and he was doing his best to ignore.

Iris gave a sharp shake of her head. 'I know you didn't. I did think about trying to find you, but we weren't in touch.' She left the words in the air and Lachlan didn't try and fill the gap with any kind of excuse. They'd both been far too hurt and heartbroken to stay in touch.

'She died around five years ago and left a whole heap of money to her remaining family, which was just my parents, my sister and myself. It seemed she didn't just own her house in Kent, she also owned one in Cornwall and one in France.'

'What?' He was shocked.

Iris laughed. 'That face. That face was exactly mine when I found out. Got to credit Aunt Lucy for playing her cards close to her chest.'

She stared down at where his hand was on hers. She didn't pull away. Just licked her lips and looked back at him. Was she feeling the sparks too—or was she just being adult about the comfort he was offering?

'So that's why I own a beautiful house in Portobello. It needed some minor updating, then I converted one of the rooms into a library.'

'You're killing me,' he groaned. It had been a dream of theirs. They'd often sent random photos from the internet to each other of beautiful libraries around the world, talking about how one day they would build one of their own. Of course, at that point, they'd also been talking about making a mini library for their kids that would take up one half of the room.

'Sorry.' But she was smiling. He could see in her eyes that she obviously loved the room.

'Dark wood or white?' It had been one of their constant debates.

She kept smiling. 'One straight wall, dark wood, specially built library shelves, and the rest of the room is painted cream. I have a pale wood floor and an oriental rug.'

'Do you have a ladder?'

She shook her head regretfully. 'Not yet. I have a stool I climb to reach the top shelves. But a ladder and chaise longue are definitely on the cards.'

There was a ping from the computer next to him, and he leaned forward and pressed the alert to see Maeve's X-ray image. He'd moved his hand automatically and now the palm of his hand felt strangely empty. He leaned forward and Iris did the same. Her shoulder brushed against his and her signature scent drifted around him again. From one comfort, to another.

'Broken rib,' they said in unison.

And it stopped them both dead.

They froze. It was something that had happened frequently, years before. But the repeat event seemed to crash around them.

It was awkward. Even uncomfortable. Because for the first time in eight years they'd actually been chatting easily, teasing each other. Being friends in a way that had existed before but had been snatched from them by their own actions.

All of a sudden Lachlan knew exactly how much had been stolen from his life.

Iris's cheeks flushed pink, as if she were just as uncomfortable as he was. Her hands folded over her chest. 'What else are you going to do for Maeve?'

Work. He was at work. His brain kicked into gear. 'I suspect she's got postural hypotension. There's a marked difference in her blood pressure when she's lying down, and when she's in a chair—that's even without standing her up.

I'll go and do a few more checks, review her current medications and take it from there. This has happened more than once.'

Iris seemed to have gathered herself and dropped back into professional mode. 'She was lucky this time with just a broken rib. It could have been her hip, her shoulder or even a head injury.'

'That's what I'm worried about. Don't worry. I'll be thorough.'

'Oh, I know you will.' There was a kind of wistful air to Iris's words as he stood up to go back to Maeve.

'You know, if she wants a female doctor instead, I'm available.' Iris's blue eyes seemed to stand out more in the bright lights of A&E, or maybe it was because of her yellow shirt. Whatever it was, it was hard to look away.

'I'll double-check with her,' he said, looking down at the tablet he'd lifted. Something sparked in his brain. 'The crew of the *McGonigal*, you heard any more about them?'

Iris gave a nod. 'The three younger crew men have all been released. The captain is still ventilated in ICU. Double pneumonia, but still fighting.'

He let out a slow breath. He knew the odds must be against the older man, but he was still here, and still fighting. 'The three young ones are lucky guys.'

She gave him a bold look. 'Must have been the exemplary care they received in *my* A&E department.'

'Must have been,' he agreed as he walked away, laughing to himself. He knew he was going to spend the next three months living down his first statement about the department.

He spent the next hour talking with Maeve, running a few more tests, taking some bloods and making a referral to another consultant. He wouldn't get to the bottom of Maeve's problem tonight. There could be an array of other issues going on—cardiac, endocrine, nervous system disorders. But he could do his best with general advice, and ways to keep her safe in the meantime while other investigations took place.

Rena appeared again. 'Want me to arrange some transportation?'

He shook his head. 'No, it's fine. I'll take her back home and make sure she's good.'

He heard a laugh and looked up. Iris was sitting next to Maeve and they were chatting, as Maeve ate some toast and drunk some tea.

Rena gave a nod. 'The smell of toast always makes Iris appear. When I make some for patients, I always make some for her too.'

Lachlan smiled, struck by the fact the team

around here knew parts of Iris like he did—even if they didn't generally say it out loud.

Rena seemed to catch his gaze. 'She's great,' she said quietly.

And before he could help it, he said, 'Just don't try and steal her raspberry ripple ice cream.'

The amused tone in his voice made Rena raise her eyebrows and smile. 'I'll remember that,' she said as she walked away.

He could have kicked himself. They'd made an agreement not to get personal at work and it felt as if he'd just stepped over that line.

Iris disappeared behind another set of curtains as he grabbed a wheelchair and went to collect Maeve.

As he helped her into the car she patted his arm. 'What a nice bunch of people you work with. All of them. And that doctor, Iris? Very pretty.'

He climbed into the driver's seat, knowing that Maeve might know more than she should. 'She's my ex-wife.'

Maeve sighed as she clicked her seat belt. 'What a fool,' she said as Lachlan reversed the car and waited for the punchline.

'What a fool she is for letting you slip through her fingers.'

Lachlan's head turned in surprise as he went

to change gear. 'That wasn't what I expected you to say.'

Maeve's eyes widened in pretend surprise. 'Oh, you thought I'd wouldn't be on your side?' She folded her hands in her lap. 'Now why would I do that? I'm Team Lachlan, as they say.'

He threw back his head and laughed. 'Team Lachlan? Where did you get that from?'

Maeve looked out the window as they started down the city streets. 'Just because I'm old doesn't mean I'm not up to date.' She gave him a wink. 'And anyhow, you're the one that walks my dog.'

'Even if he hates me.' Lachlan smiled.

'I think he's warming to you.' Maeve was still watching out the dark windows. 'And just for the record, even though I'm Team Lachlan, I still liked her.'

He glanced sideways, but Maeve's eyes were elsewhere, and somehow he knew she wouldn't let this go.

CHAPTER FOUR

IRIS WAS UNSETTLED. She couldn't help it. Lachlan Brodie was getting under her skin.

Truth was, he'd never really stopped getting under her skin. But having a clean break and being away from him had felt like the right move at the time.

They'd spent a few months still working in close proximity after their initial split, but both had found it too hard. All they did was fight. Pent-up resentment and frustration never did any workplace any good. So, they'd both decided to play at being grown-ups.

Neither had really wanted to leave the huge A&E they worked at in London. But they'd each applied for other jobs. Iris had gone to Melbourne, Australia, for six months, and Lachlan had gone to San Francisco. And after that, she'd lost track of him.

That had been a conscious decision on her part. Iris had been full of regrets, mainly about how she'd coped with things going wrong and the arguments they'd had. It was harder still having to admit to being at fault for some of it. That was a hurdle that had taken a few years to settle in her brain. So many choices made— or refused—and so many what-ifs to come to terms with.

They'd both been far too young to get married, their romance and wedding a whirlwind. They'd barely had time to get to know each other properly before things had started falling apart. Their dreams of a family had led them to start trying for one almost immediately, with all the heartache that had led to. They'd barely celebrated their third wedding anniversary by the time they'd admitted it was over.

Truth was, she'd never in a million years expected Lachlan to turn up in her A&E, and one sight of him had clean taken her breath away.

Sure, he'd insulted her immediately and they'd fought. And even though she'd told him and herself that they'd only reached a mutual agreement for him to stay because she was so desperate for good staff, her own brain kept screaming at her, *That's not true!*

Because whilst seeing Lachlan again was like a punch to the chest, it was also a permanent ache in her soul. Now she was reminded on a daily basis what might have been.

And that made her feel even more guilty. Of course, if she'd stayed with Lachlan, she would never have come to Ireland, made it her home and adopted Holly. She couldn't ever have a single doubt about the best thing that had happened in her life.

But her life, which had felt so put together for the last few years, now seemed to be unravelling again inside her head.

She'd tried to date. But her heart had never been truly in it. She just thought the timing had been off, or she hadn't quite met the right man. But Lachlan constantly being around now was telling her exactly why.

Because none of the men had ever measured up to Lachlan.

The chat they'd had last week when he'd showed up unexpectedly with his neighbour had pulled so many of the familiar strings in her that she hadn't been able to stop playing it over and over in her head.

On the shifts they did together, she could see even more glances between staff. Lachlan and Iris were in sync. They always had been when they'd worked together. It brought out the best in both of them.

Today, he hadn't been working, but something had been niggling away at her.

'Iris?' One of the secretaries tapped her on

the shoulder. 'You'd asked me to pull some records from other A&E departments?'

She nodded and took the files. Records in their department were all digital and sometimes it took a little time to get paper records from other parts of the city.

She glanced down and read for a few minutes. 'Does anyone know where Lachlan is today?' The blank looks around her told her everything she needed to know.

He'd flagged something to her a few days ago. An unusual infection in a teenager. Iris had just seen something similar and asked the secretary to make some calls around other A&E departments in the city. Now, she just needed to put the pieces together, and Lachlan would be the best person to help her.

She called up to HR, asking for his mobile phone number. They handed it over but when she called it didn't connect. Sighing, she tried to rack her brains. He was off duty. He'd told her the cottage phone line had gone down in the storms. So, she checked Maeve's record and dialled her listed mobile instead. Maeve answered the phone within a few rings. 'Maeve Corwin speaking.'

'Hi, Mrs Corwin, this is Dr Conway from St Mary's calling—Iris. I hope you don't mind, but I'm trying to get hold of Lachlan. I know the phone line to his cottage is down—would you happen to know where he is?'

If Maeve was surprised at Iris's call, she didn't let on. Instead, she gave a gentle laugh. 'On a day like this? There's only one place that man would be. The Trinity Library, of course.' She paused for a few seconds and then added, 'I thought you might have guessed that one.'

Her insides squirmed. Of course. She should have known. 'I guess I'm a little out of touch,' she admitted, without saying anything more. From Maeve's earlier comment she was guessing Lachlan had mentioned they had history together.

'Nothing wrong with getting back into touch,' said Maeve mischievously, before replacing the phone.

Iris smiled and shook her head, glancing at the clock. She was officially off duty. She turned to Ryan. 'I'm going to see if I can find Lachlan and try and figure out something about a few patients. We might be back in later.'

Ryan looked poised to say something, but then pressed his lips together and gave a nod. 'No problem.'

Iris changed quickly and walked to the car park, snaking her way through the city traffic towards Trinity College.

It was a beautiful day and she knew there

would be a queue of visitors waiting to visit the Book of Kells exhibition and great long room of the famous library. So, Iris pulled out her phone and booked her admission online. She was lucky; she could get in soon, and save waiting in the long queue.

She waited for her time, then showed her pass and walked straight in, passing quickly through the front entrance.

She entered through the dark wood doors and immediately looked upwards at the barrel-vaulted ceiling, inhaling deeply the scent of the ancient leather-bound books. She would never get tired of that. There were benches at either end of the middle of the long room, with green ropes keeping the two hundred thousand previous books safely out of reach. Marble busts lined the length of the long room's two-storey main chamber, as if keeping guard of the rows of books at their entrance points. Aristotle, Homer, Shakespeare and Socrates were all on duty, with high oak shelves behind them, varying in number, books crammed together and a long metal ladder to assist those important enough to touch the previous volumes.

The room was busy, with several older citizens just sitting on the benches that resembled old church pews and gazing up at the ceiling and second floor.

Iris gave herself a moment. It had been a few years since she'd been here. With work, and Holly, there just hadn't been the time. She smiled as she started to walk slowly along the rows. At any point she could lean forward a little and try to make out the faded text on some of the ancient books, wondering at the titles and what information lay beneath the covers. This place really was a wonder.

Voices were hushed as this was every book lover's dream. She wished she could actually sit down in here for a whole day and study. Instead, there were other parts of the library for that, as this long room and the exhibition was one of Dublin's top tourist attractions.

Iris wove her way through the crowds, scanning for Lachlan's dark hair. Eventually she glimpsed his broad shoulders, dressed in a pale blue shirt, his short dark curls bringing a smile to her face as she made her way towards him. He was next to the bust of Sir Isaac Newton, doing much as she'd done a few moments earlier, and squinting at some of the book titles. She could see his phone in one hand where he'd taken a few notes of titles, and he had a book of his own tucked under one arm.

She gave him a gentle nudge. 'Guess your phone doesn't get a signal in a place like this?'

He started and turned towards her, surprise

written all over his face. But it only took a few seconds for the edges of his mouth to turn upwards. 'Switched the ringer off anyway,' he admitted. 'This is hallowed ground.' He turned the phone towards her, so she could see there was absolutely no signal in here at all. His brow creased. 'Is something wrong?'

She waggled her hand. 'I'm not sure. I wanted to talk to you about the case you mentioned to me a few days ago. There's been a few more. Can we grab a coffee?'

'Sure,' he said quickly, and gestured for her to head to the exit.

'Sorry to ruin your day,' she said over her shoulder as they headed to the exit.

He waved his hand. 'No worries. I was only going to sit outside somewhere with my book for a bit. Then, of course, go back and walk Scout, who maybe only hates me about eighty-five percent right now.'

She laughed. 'Maeve's dog hates you?'

'Of course. By the time I wear him down, either me or him will be heading for the Pearly Gates.'

'Don't tell me you created the same bad impression with him that you did at the hospital?'

Lachlan put his hand to his chest and had the cheek to look offended. 'Me? Create a bad impression? No.' He shook his head. 'That was just timing, and shock.'

'Shock at seeing me?'

They weaved their way out of the exit and across the grass towards the nearest street lined with coffee shops. 'It's not every day your ex turns up.'

She shook her finger at him. 'Oh, no, it wasn't me who turned up. It was you. Invading my little space with your big hair.'

He caught a glimpse of himself in a shop window. 'What's wrong with the hair? Too long already?'

It had been a constant joke when they were married. Cut short, his hair had just a hint of the dark curls. Left any longer the curls seemed to multiply in space and volume overnight, making Lachlan's hair the butt of many jokes.

She'd always dreamed of having a little girl with dark curls like Lachlan's, and a pang of sorrow twisted inside her. It had been a long time since she'd thought like that.

'Your hair is fine,' she said a bit more sharply than she meant to. He gave her a curious stare and directed her towards a coffee shop with tables and chairs outside in the sun.

They waited a few moments for a young waitress to take their order. Iris went to the nearby display cabinet to pick a cake, but Lach-

Ian did what he always did. 'A coffee and a doughnut, whatever you've got.'

She smiled again. 'Still with the doughnuts?'

'Why not? They're good in any shape or form—jam, custard, apple, plain, iced.' He smiled. 'I could go on for ever.'

'I thought your cake selection might have improved over time.'

'Why fix what's not broken?' There was an awkward silence between them. It was clear their minds had just gone back to their own, very broken previous relationship. But this was about doughnuts. Not about them.

'I got a bacon doughnut once.' Lachlan was obviously trying to fill the silence.

She wrinkled her nose. 'Where on earth did you get that?'

'America. I was working in an ER, and a bakery around the corner started doing bacon doughnuts. It became the standard breakfast food.'

'I'm surprised you didn't stay.' She couldn't help it. She was curious about where he'd been, even though she didn't want to be.

He paused as the coffee and cakes were sat down by the waitress. 'I thought about it. The career opportunities were good, but after a while, I wanted to go back to England.'

'Where did you go?'

This time when he looked at her, she saw something in those brown eyes. Something that he clearly didn't want to share. She glanced down at the strawberry tart she'd ordered and wondered how on earth she could eat it without getting sauce everywhere. It seemed easier to concentrate on that than anything else.

He didn't answer the question, just moved smoothly onto something else. 'So, what is it you wanted to talk about?'

She pulled out her phone and showed him the notes she'd taken. 'You remember that kid you saw a few days ago—the one with nothing you really could put your finger on?'

His forehead creased. 'Yeah, the seventeen-year-old with the minor temperature and muscle aches. He definitely wasn't telling me everything, and I couldn't really treat him with so little to go on.' He groaned and leaned back. 'Don't tell me, he's back and I missed something.'

She shook her head. 'No, but we've had a few other teenagers all reporting similar symptoms across the city in the last two days.'

'What have they been up to?'

She leaned her head on her hand as she tried to break up her strawberry tart with a fork. 'And why didn't they just to go to their GP?'

'So, what are you thinking?' he asked.

'I'm thinking that there could be more to this than meets the eye.'

Lachlan took a bite of his doughnut. 'The most obvious thing for teenagers is glandular fever, but it doesn't fit.'

'No, it doesn't.'

Lachlan pointed to a newspaper headline at the shop next door. 'What about that?'

Iris turned her head. '"*Spate of break-ins at designer properties.*"' She raised her eyebrows. 'That's close to your new neck of the woods. How can they be connected?'

'Because the radio this morning said the police suspect teenagers. There's been some minor damage, but at most of the break-ins it's been consumption of alcohol and use of the property that seems to have been the main motivation.'

Iris gave a slow nod. 'It could be. But does that mean there's something toxic at one of those houses?' She pulled a face. 'Or illegal? Are we going down the entirely wrong route?'

Her phone rang and she answered quickly, her eyes gleaming as she looked at Lachlan. 'Fergus, I think I love you. I'm with Dr Brodie now. We were just discussing the cases. We'll be in soon.'

Lachlan was already grabbing for his wallet to pay the bill when Iris stopped abruptly. 'What's wrong?' he asked.

She took a moment, then gave him a serious glance. 'I'm sorry, it's your day off, and you clearly had plans.' Her eyes went to the book grasped in his other hand. 'I shouldn't have assumed you would be happy to work without checking first.'

He gave her an amused smile. 'As long as I'm back later to walk Scout, my day is yours.' He settled the bill and turned to her. 'Besides, you've already worked today, shouldn't you be worrying about yourself?'

She looked at the clock on her phone screen and grimaced. Holly was due out of school soon. She'd be picked up by the childminder, but this could take longer than the childminder usually stayed. 'Give me two minutes to make a call, then we can head to the hospital in my car. Or—' she glanced around at the streets that were full of parked cars '—did you bring your own?'

He shook his head. 'I took the DART today. Decided to be a cross between a local and a tourist.' He took a few steps away. 'You make your call and I'll wait for you.'

She was grateful he gave her a little space, conscious that at some point she should really mention Holly. It was beginning to feel a bit awkward—all on her side, of course. But she just didn't want to start arguing again with Lachlan. Telling him she'd adopted a child on her own would bring up a whole conversation, a whole pile of feelings that she just wasn't comfortable discussing with him. He'd likely be hurt—maybe even angry—and it felt as if she and Lachlan were just reaching a place she'd never imagined they could get to: friends. Plus, he was only here for three months, and a few of those weeks had passed already. Was it really worth telling him something that might cause a huge amount of tension between them for the rest of his stay?

She'd been well aware she wasn't the only one with a broken heart when they'd split. She was treading carefully, but it seemed as if Lachlan had reached some equilibrium in his life. Would admitting she'd moved on from their marriage, and created a family of her own without him, be like rubbing salt in an old wound? She certainly didn't want to do that to him.

Once she finished her call they walked quickly to her small red car. She laughed as he folded his long legs into it. 'You realise you've set the hares running already,' he said.

'What do you mean?' She pulled out into the city traffic.

'You told Fergus you were with me. People

will wonder why you're spending time with me when we're not working.' There was a hint of amusement in his voice.

She raised an eyebrow at his teasing. 'I already told Ryan I was coming to find you, and if anyone else asks, I'll be just as honest. The case that annoyed you, started to annoy me too. I dug a little deeper and thought it was worth trying to join the dots.'

'So, what does Fergus have for us? I take it another case has come in?'

'A case that was seen yesterday at Dublin Memorial has presented at St Mary's. Fergus gave me a call, because I'd told anyone to let me know if we got any further cases. According to him, this kid has taken a downhill turn.'

'Let's try and get a better history. I think the young guy that I saw wasn't entirely truthful about where he'd been. It might give us a clue to whether this is actually some kind of disease, infection or an environmental thing.'

They chatted easily as they reached the hospital, pulling into the staff car park. Part of her insides were glowing. For a few moments she'd cursed herself for making assumptions about Lachlan wanting to come back into work—she had no right to do that any more. But when she'd stopped, and corrected herself, he'd been only too happy to help—just like he'd always been. Over their eight years apart, there had been major changes in her life; she suspected there might have been major changes in his too. But it was still good to know that, at heart, Lachlan seemed the same man.

Fergus looked up as they entered A&E. He gave the two of them a half-knowing smile. 'Good, you're here.' He looked at them both, 'Want to get changed, or just want to see the patient?'

Iris glanced down at her white trousers and pink shirt, knowing just how much she should get changed, but Lachlan laughed and gave her a nudge. 'Go on, take a chance. Risk it.'

She sighed. 'Who needs white trousers any-how?' she asked as they both washed up at one of the nearby sinks.

Fergus took them into one of the cubicles. 'This is Tyler Brooks. He's seventeen and pre-sented an hour ago, with a temp of thirty-nine, a dry cough, headache, muscle pains and short-ness of breath. I've taken some bloods and he's had a chest X-ray…just waiting for the results. He was sent home last night from Dublin Me-morial with no treatment, but his symptoms weren't as bad last night. He also reports a few episodes of D&V at home. I gave him some paracetamol for his temperature.'

The young man looked completely worn out.

He was attached to a standard monitor and had a probe on his finger and an oxygen mask on his face.

Lachlan stood at the edge of the trolley. 'Hi, Tyler,' he said quietly. 'I'm Dr Brodie and this is Dr Conway. We've seen a few sick teenagers in the last couple of days, and we're trying to find out why.'

Tyler's eyes flew open and he instantly looked scared. Lachlan put his hands up. 'I'm not here to get you into trouble. I just want to find out what's wrong with you.'

Iris moved around the other side of the trolley. 'Do you mind if I have a listen to your chest?'

Tyler shook his head and Iris listened to the front and then the back, shooting a look at Lachlan. This young man's lungs sounded far from good. She'd guess at the least he had pneumonia, which was unusual for someone this age.

She lifted his chart. 'Can I just double-check? No history of asthma, or any chest complaints?'

Tyler shook his head, then started to cough. She saw something flare in Lachlan's eyes at the sound of the cough.

He waited until the coughing stopped, then spoke quietly to Tyler again. 'Have you been somewhere different in the last few days?'

Tyler shot him a glance, and Lachlan didn't need the answer out loud.

'Okay, so is there a chance you touched something you shouldn't have? Chemicals, gardening supplies?'

Tyler closed his eyes again, clearly exhausted. 'We didn't touch anything like that. Just had a few drinks, and went in the hot tub,' he sighed.

Hot tub. Lachlan's vision connected with hers. 'Is it a hot tub you'd been in before?' he asked.

Tyler shook his head again. Lachlan patted his arm. 'I think we might know what's wrong with you. Let us check your blood results and chest X-ray and we'll be back in a minute.'

They walked to the nurses' station and pulled up the chest X-ray. Tyler's lungs showed signs of pneumonia, with consolidation at the bottom of both lungs.

'Want to take a guess at his bloods?' asked Lachlan.

Iris pulled them up and nodded as she looked at them. 'All abnormal, low sodium levels overall.'

'He has legionnaire's disease.' They both nodded at each other.

Lachlan started pulling up another record. 'Do you think the other kids might have had Pontiac fever? It's the same disease, just milder.'

She looked at the notes on her phone. 'It could be.' She glanced anxiously back to the cubicle. 'But there could be more that have legionnaire's—likely from that hot tub. We might not have seen them yet.'

Lachlan looked thoughtful. 'The police should know which of the houses that were broken into had hot tubs. If they'd been sealed up while the owners aren't there, and the kids just fired it on without knowing any of the treatments to use, it's likely that's where they've picked up the disease.' He gave her a smile. 'How about I deal with Tyler, and you talk to environmental health and the police?' He gave a small shrug. 'I figure you know more people around here than I do.'

She picked up a phone. 'And I figure you want the easy bit, instead of all the paperwork.' They were teasing each other again.

He picked up Tyler's chart and walked back towards the bay. 'Some people might think that you know me,' he quipped over his shoulder, and threw her a wink.

The easy remark let a whole warmness spread over her body. Reaching parts that she'd forgotten she possessed for quite a while. She looked down and her hand started to tremble. Once it started, it didn't stop.

Iris quickly checked to see no one was

watching her and hurried along to the changing room, closing the door behind her and leaning against it.

Her heart was clamouring in her chest.

Tears brimmed in her eyes. This was ridiculous. Ludicrous. They'd had a fairly normal couple of weeks working together. Her heart told her they were on their way to being friends. They were even beginning to joke around each other.

She sucked in a breath and started coughing. All the stuff that she'd kept deep down inside her for years was trying to push its way to the surface. And all it had taken was an off-the-cuff remark from her ex, about what people might say about them.

No one else in the world would get this. She couldn't explain this rush of emotions if she tried. But that cheeky glance, those casual words and that blooming wink had sparked more memories than anything else had.

Because that's how life had used to be between them. And she'd never, ever met anyone else who had made her feel the way that Lachlan had.

It had taken her right back. Way, way back to the start of their relationship when they were so in sync. When every time she glanced at Lach-

Ian Brodie her heart skipped a couple of beats. When even a brush of a hand could make them want to head to the nearest room with a locking door. When she felt totally loved, adored and safe around him. When the whole of their lives stretched out for them like a beautiful winding path they would walk together.

Of course, there were a few things she hadn't told him. Everything had seemed so instantly good between them that she hadn't wanted to tell him anything that might make him think less of her. So, although he knew she was adopted, she didn't tell him the true relationship between herself and her adopted parents. She didn't tell him how abandoned she'd felt when their newly conceived baby had been born, how useless and unworthy—or how much she'd played up for attention, making everything worse. He hadn't asked too many questions. Particularly about how her parents hadn't come to their wedding. She'd made a few half-hearted excuses about Australia being too far away, and how they'd married at such short notice, that there hadn't really been time to make arrangements.

Guilt threatened to swamp her. Guilt that she'd kept secrets. Guilt that her driven obsession of starting their own family had ultimately driven them apart. Guilt that she'd ruined their relationship and their future.

No. No. Iris took some deep breaths and started to think rationally. She pressed her hand against her heart, which was still beating too fast.

Life had taken them in different directions. Yes, she'd missed his company, his love and the life they'd had together. But she couldn't go back. *They* couldn't go back.

And the most ridiculous thing was she didn't even know if he would want to. She was being pathetic. One wink, and a smart remark, and she was in the changing rooms, crying like a baby.

But the attraction was still there for her. Those knowing brown eyes had seen too much of Iris. They'd seen her at her worst, and at her best, and she couldn't pretend that a tingle hadn't shot up her arm when he'd touched her when they were talking about Aunt Lucy. The feel of his skin against hers…

She shook herself. She couldn't allow herself to go back to that place. It was torture to her. Torture to remember what she'd lost, and to see it walking around in front of her again. She was trying so, so hard to be a grown-up about this.

She wiped her eyes, starting to get angry with herself. She had a job to do. She had a child to get home to. A daughter who loved her, was definitely the boss and regularly told her off.

Maybe Lachlan working here wasn't such a good idea after all. Yes, they'd got to the bottom of something today, in a way that was so familiar to her. That's all this was. She was having a weird, momentary flashback, because they'd relived how well their working relationship used to be. But in the scale of life, it was nothing.

She wiped her eyes and washed her hands, checking her appearance in the mirror and putting on some lipstick. She still had those calls to make. There could be other kids in this city who'd been exposed to legionella.

She wasn't worried about Tyler. Lachlan would have started him on the right treatment and taken care of him. She had no doubts about his abilities as a doctor. But she needed to find out if he'd got a better history of where those kids had been.

She took a deep breath and walked out to find him. 'Any idea where the house with the hot tub is yet?'

He was typing up some notes as he started speaking. 'I think it might be the one close to where that rock star lives.' He looked up. 'Iris? What's wrong?'

Darn it. She pressed her lips together. 'Nothing's wrong.' Her tone was dismissive because she couldn't handle this conversation now.

He looked at her strangely, then turned over a chart and scribbled something on the back. 'Here, Tyler roughly told me where they drove to. I don't know that part of the area too well. You might have a better idea.'

She stared down at the pencilled map and nodded. 'This will do.'

She went to walk away but Lachlan grabbed her arm. Concern was written all over his face. 'You would tell me if something was wrong, wouldn't you?'

She held her breath, looking at those dark brown eyes again. The ones she used to love and trust with her whole heart.

She blinked and straightened. 'No,' she answered truthfully, not reacting to the surprise on his face. 'We're long past that part of our lives.'

Then she turned on her heel and walked away, ignoring the fact that she knew he was watching every step she took.

CHAPTER FIVE

LACHLAN BRODIE HAD no idea what was going on in his life.

He'd found a perfectly nice cottage to stay in. He was loving the ability to tramp over the fields with Scout and keep an eye on Maeve while her medications were reviewed and she was undergoing a few other tests.

In theory, work was going well. The fire in his belly had been well and truly lit again working in Dublin's A&E. He'd talked to the four other A&E departments around the city, and they'd developed better ways to flag children who presented frequently across all five hospitals after working alongside their IT colleagues.

It was a system used in other cities he'd worked in, and had been one of the first things he'd thought about since being back. In a world dominated by IT now, all A&E departments should talk easily to each other, but it didn't always happen. Lachlan hated to think of a kid with bruises being taken to one hospital, then presenting at another with a broken bone, and no one connecting the dots. The staff around him had been enthusiastic; all he'd had to do was present the system, and gain some permissions to use it. After that, it had been adopted easily, and he was proud.

He was fast becoming enamoured by this beautiful city and its people. He loved being so close to the sea. The area around the harbourside was becoming a favourite. A few of the other doctors had invited him out for drinks at the local pubs and to join their football team.

In lots of ways, he was enjoying his time here. Except for one thing. The giant, beautiful thorn in his side that was Iris Conway.

He had absolutely no idea what was going in inside her head.

One minute, he'd thought they were on their way to being friends. The sparks were still there. Although she was eight years older, and—just like him—had a few little lines around her face, she was every bit as attractive as she'd always been. At times when they chatted things felt so natural. So…before.

Before all the issues that had driven them apart. He wished he could turn back the clock. He wished he'd been more direct with her. He would have done anything to keep her happy back then, so he'd agreed with all the avenues she wanted to pursue and those she hadn't. They'd both had dreams of a family, and she'd been determined to never put those aside.

But, with time and retrospective thinking, Lachlan wished he hadn't been so obliging. He wished he'd sat his wife down and told her to stop. Told her over and over that *she* would always be enough for him. That, just them, growing old together, was his happy-ever-after. Children would have been a welcome addition, but not an essential part of their future together.

And he had tried to say those words to her. But they had been lost in amongst the tears and fights. Now, when he looked at Iris, he saw eight years that he had lost with the woman that had once owned his whole heart.

He had never really verbalised to Iris how much of the blame he'd felt for their break-up. He realised now he'd spent way too much time talking about how much he wanted a big family: a couple of boys who might look like him, a couple of girls who would look like Iris. They'd also, in their youth and inexperience, dreamed of names for those children, with imaginary personality traits. All of that was wonderful, until the harsh wake-up call that their dreams wouldn't become reality. He'd known she was adopted, and hadn't pushed when she'd rejected the suggestion to try that route themselves.

Hindsight was a wonderful thing, and he knew now that there were lots of conversations they hadn't managed to have that they should have had. And that still bothered him. He should have encouraged her to talk to him about adoption. But every word had seemed to hurt her without him trying, and he would always regret letting her walk away when she wanted to. Maybe if they'd been older, married longer—maybe if they'd had a bit more life experience—they would have had more resilience to weather the storm of infertility. But it was far too late now.

Even though he knew Iris would always hold a part of his heart.

As all his regrets played out in his head, he wondered if they might ever have these conversations out loud, as older, wiser individuals. But where on earth would they have them? In the staff room? On the stairs between floors?

Part of him wondered if it was stupid to think like that. Rehashing the past wouldn't help anyone.

Yet at times when their gazes meshed, it felt like whole other conversations were going on.

It all seemed so random. Him, turning up here, and seeing Iris again after all this time.

Realising the connection that had once been between them still seemed as if it were there.

But for the last few weeks, Iris had been colder towards him. She'd tried to distance herself from him. There was no laughing, no casual conversations, and every time he watched her walk in another direction, deliberately avoiding him, a little part inside him died.

His house phone rang and he answered quickly. 'Hi, it's Rena. Don't suppose you can cover at short notice?'

'Sure, what's wrong?'

'Ryan's wife has gone into labour. Only a week early, but he needs to leave.'

Lachlan felt a little pang inside him. 'Aww, of course. Wish him well from me. I'll leave in the next five minutes.'

He grabbed a few things and made a quick call to Maeve to check she didn't need anything before he left. It was a Tuesday night. He could literally toss a coin to see if it would be busy tonight or not. Generally, Thursday to Sunday night shifts were always busy, but Monday to Wednesday could be a hit or a miss. Quiet shifts were a killer. Lachlan wasn't good at sitting still.

By the time he reached the department he was reassured that there were only a few people in the waiting room. As he walked through the department he blinked in surprise as he noticed Iris in the plaster cast room, winding a fibreglass cast around a woman's wrist.

'Hey,' he said.

'Oh, you're here.' She didn't sound exactly happy to see him. He hadn't expected her to be the other doctor on duty—there were always at least two, but somehow he guessed she might have tried everyone else before him.

'No problem,' he said. 'Where do you want me?'

'Now there's a question,' the female patient responded quickly with laughter in her voice.

Iris's cheeks flamed and she shook her head without meeting his gaze. 'Can you just deal with the cases on the board?'

'No problem.' It was a less than stellar handover. But Lachlan was more than capable of filling in where required.

He quickly checked over a kid with a football injury, an older man with a swollen ankle and a very angry baby with colic. The mother was tearful and upset, mainly at the thought of being powerless to control her child's symptoms and blaming herself for wasting A&E staff's time.

Lachlan recognised instantly she needed some time out. He spoke to Rena, who was still on duty, and got her to show the mum to the canteen to get something to eat, while he paced the corridor with the screaming baby on his shoulder.

He watched as Iris dispatched the woman with the purple cast before she strode down the corridor towards him.

'What's going on?' She looked mildly irritated.

Lachlan swapped the little boy onto his other shoulder. 'I'm taking a turn holding little angry Aiden here, so his mum can get some peace. He's been like this for over an hour.' He rubbed the baby's back. 'I imagine he'll do much better in a month's time when he's old enough to start weaning, but until then...'

Iris put her own hand onto the baby's back and looked up and down the corridor. 'Go on, then. I'll take a turn too.'

'Are you sure?'

'Don't look so shocked.' She looked at Aiden again with a hesitant smile. 'Boy, can this little fellow scream.'

'Oh, yes,' laughed Lachlan, 'which is why I thought mum needed a break.'

She lifted the baby from his arms and adjusted him onto her shoulder. Aiden continued to scream. 'Okay, you make the coffee. There's doughnuts in the staff room.'

He gave her a sideways glance. 'Anyone would think you knew I'd be working.'

She rolled her eyes. 'Ryan brought them in tonight. He wasn't expecting to get called away.' Then she grinned wickedly. 'I am going to torment him all night by sending him pictures every time a doughnut leaves the box, all whilst his wife is in labour. It will send him quietly mad.'

'Now that's just mean.'

'Just the A&E way of life,' she said as she started down the corridor, rubbing Aiden's back and whispering quietly in his ear.

By the time Lachlan had made the coffee, Iris had managed to quieten Aiden. She walked back into the room tugging a wheeled crib behind her and looking critically around the room. 'Mind if I put the lights down a bit?'

He shook his head. 'You must have the magic touch.' The words came out easily, and then he cringed a little, realising how that could feel for a woman who'd wanted a family.

But Iris didn't seem to notice. 'No magic touch,' she said as she laid him down in the crib and lowered the lights. 'I strongly suspect he's just exhausted himself.'

She sat down next to Lachlan and reached for her coffee, letting out a sigh.

He could almost hear the silence echoing

around them. He took a sideways glance. Iris had her hair in her usual ponytail and was wearing pale blue scrubs. She had some light make-up on her face and looked a little tired.

He took a deep breath, wondering where to start. 'I like Dublin.'

'You do?' She seemed surprised by that statement.

He nodded. 'It's a beautiful city. Lots of character. The people too, they're very welcoming.'

She took a sip of her coffee. 'Sounds like you want to stay.'

'I might.'

Iris froze. He knew that he'd taken her by surprise. But she also knew he only had a three-month contract right now.

He moved, turning to face her on the central chairs. 'But it feels like yours.'

It was best just to say it out loud.

She frowned. 'What do you mean—it's mine?'

He shrugged his shoulders. 'It is. It's your city. You've been here a while. You're head of this department. You bought a house and built a library.' He gave a gentle laugh. 'For anyone that knows you, that's pretty much a sign you plan on staying here long-term.'

She bit her bottom lip, watching him carefully. 'I do,' she agreed. 'I like it here. But I can't put my name on a city and call it my own.'

He felt his heart break a little at the way she said those words, reading everything she wasn't saying out loud. This was her place. And he was likely outstaying his welcome. Just as well he'd already agreed to a new contract somewhere else.

'We both know that if I'd known you were here, I wouldn't have taken this job.' It didn't sound nice saying it out loud. But he was only being honest for them both. 'It was never my intention to appear unannounced.' He lowered his gaze. 'I honestly didn't think we'd run into each other again.'

'Nor did I,' she agreed quietly.

His arm was on the back of the chair between them. 'So, what now?'

He looked back up and held her gaze. Lachlan could almost swear there was a giant ticking clock somewhere in the room, counting out the seconds of silence in the loudest possible way.

'I don't know,' she finally whispered.

'Do you hate me being around?'

'No' was her immediate reaction, but then he saw her take another breath. 'And yes,' she added.

It was painful. Just the way he thought it would be. She was slowly cutting thin wafers of his heart and tossing them away. But the way she was looking at him told him something else. Even though the lights were dim, he was sure his eyes weren't playing tricks. She was looking at him as if...

Her voice was husky. 'It's confusing,' she murmured. '*You're* confusing.'

He shifted a little, subconsciously getting a little closer. Her blue eyes were on his.

'How do I confuse you?'

She gave a soft smile. 'Because sometimes I just hear your voice, sense your presence or listen to your laugh, and it takes me back to a whole other world.'

'I know the feeling,' he replied in a low voice. 'I never expected...' His words tailed off, unsure if he should actually say what he was thinking out loud.

'To see me again?'

He gave a little laugh but shook his head. 'Well, there was obviously *that*.'

'But?' There was a hopeful edge to her voice that he just couldn't ignore. Not when it was just them. Not when they were here like this.

He held his palms upwards. 'I just never expected this again.' He kept his eyes fixed on hers. He had no idea how she felt about all this. He knew it confused every part of him. He couldn't be sure that he was reading things right. He knew that he found Iris every bit as attractive as he ever had. He knew that any time he was around her, he itched to get closer. Just to be nearer, just to be in her presence. Was he crazy? Because it was starting to feel like he was.

But Iris's pale blue eyes held his gaze. He watched her nervously swallow. 'What is this?' she whispered.

He dropped his gaze and shook his head as the low laughter bubbled again. 'I'm darned if I know.'

She shifted next to him. He hadn't meant to make her feel uncomfortable. 'I can go,' he said quickly. 'And I will go. I've agreed to a three-month contract in Glasgow after this.'

'You have?' There was a small hint of panic in that response. And before she knew it, Iris had reached out to him. The warm palm of her hand pressed down on his bare arm. He was almost scared to look at their skin-on-skin contact. Scared of how easily it made his heartbeat quicken and his pulse feel as if it echoed in his ears. His heart was contracting so hard he knew he had to speak. He had to say some of the words out loud. He could sense an air of desperation about her, and he understood it, because he felt it too.

'I only ever wanted you to be happy, Iris.'

Her fingers tightened on his arm and he looked up to see a single tear fall down her cheek. 'I know that…' Her voice shook and he pulled her into his arms.

His reactions were automatic. Iris's tears had always broken him. The sense of heat against him was intense. Her head nuzzled into his neck, and her arms wove around his waist, clinging on tight.

For a few moments, they stayed like that. That closeness, those curves against the lines of his body, reminded him of how much they'd always felt like a perfect match. No one had ever invoked the same kind of sensations in him that Iris did. They had seemed to connect in a way he'd just never managed with anyone else.

As he breathed in, he inhaled her scent. Not just her perfume, but the shampoo in her hair and the soap on her skin. Tingles shot across the surface of his skin. He gave a little groan. 'Iris,' was all he managed to say.

It was as if the sound of her name set her alight. She lifted her head with a gleam of determination in her eyes. She shifted position so quickly he didn't even have time to think, kneeling astride him and moving her lips to his.

If Lachlan had been trying to keep things subdued and controlled, that was all out of the window now. He matched her kiss for kiss, hungrier for her by the second, his hand sliding up the inside of her scrub top and up the length of her back.

Iris couldn't get any closer, but she tried. Sliding her fingers through his hair, laughing as he let out another groan, then clasping the back of his neck as she ran kisses down the side of his face.

'I had to know,' she said breathlessly as she kept kissing him.

'Had to know what?' He wasn't really paying attention to the words, as he was far too distracted by what her hands were doing now.

She nibbled at his ear. 'Had to know if it was still there. Still us.'

He couldn't help his deep throaty laugh. 'Oh, it's still there. You can't deny that chemistry.' Relief and heat were igniting every cell in his body. He wasn't crazy, and he hadn't imagined it. This was every bit as real as he thought it was. *Too* real, in fact.

But Iris pulled back and closed her eyes. She looked every bit as overwhelmed as he felt right now. It was almost like she was trying to catch her breath and collect her thoughts. Lachlan pulled her towards him again.

A little murmur sounded behind them.

They both froze. Lachlan was sure he could hear their hearts beating above any other noise.

After a few frozen moments he let out a strangled whisper. 'Scared to move.'

Her head was right next to his ear. 'You should be.' Her voice was barely audible. 'Little guy is looking me straight in the eye.'

Lachlan started to laugh too, his chest reverberating against hers. 'I guess you can say we were caught red-handed.'

She gave a half-hearted smile and swung her leg back over and slid on to the chair next to him. 'I'm innocent. I was just trying to get closer to the jam doughnuts.'

There was a pang deep down inside him. He wanted to *talk* to her. And he could sense Iris retreating again. Their chemistry was electric, but it was clear there was still so much of herself she wanted to keep hidden from him.

He'd been burned before. They both had. And the truth was, Lachlan wasn't sure he could go through that again. It had been too hard, too painful, to get over. He'd spent the last eight years trying to replace what he'd lost, without success.

Reigniting the fire again could cause even more damage. He wasn't sure how much he could hold together if things between him and Iris backfired as spectacularly as they had before. The vibe he was getting right now was that Iris was still the same person. Still someone who didn't want to dig too deep, and be really, really honest about things. He couldn't let his heart get tangled up with her again. Not unless she could be more open with him.

'What is this, Iris?'

The humour left her eyes. She knew exactly what he was getting at. He didn't need to spell it out for her.

Iris paused and the wait seemed to be killing parts of him.

She looked down at her hands. 'I don't know. So much has happened. There's a lot about me you don't know.'

His stomach muscles clenched. He had to resist the urge to offer platitudes or say anything that made him sound the way he really felt like now. No. He was long since done being that person around Iris. He took a deep breath. 'I'm only here for another—what? Seven weeks? There's chemistry between us. That's never changed. So, why don't we just take the opportunity to enjoy it?'

Short term. With no long-term damage. He could do that. But that was about all he could do.

Iris stood up. He could tell she was considering saying no. So, he reached out his hand and took hers gently. 'It's fine,' he said gently. He couldn't pretend that every cell in his body wasn't currently been driven crazy by the hormones racing around his system. That kiss with Iris had reignited something in him.

She shook her head. 'No… I don't think I can do this.'

But while she said it, her blue eyes met his gaze, and she stopped holding his hand and instead threaded her fingers through his, giving him a little tug towards her.

'Okay,' he said slowly, 'I'm getting mixed messages here. Because I can't read you any more, Iris,' he admitted. 'I sometimes wonder if I ever could. You need to tell me what you want.' He couldn't keep the sadness out of his words. Because it was there. And he didn't feel the need to hide it from her.

'You could always read me, Lachlan.' Her voice was hoarse. 'Often better than I could myself.' She was staring straight into his eyes, and he wondered if this was it. A repeat of past history. Another chance to walk away.

'Kiss me,' she said suddenly.

He blinked. He'd thought she was going to move. He'd thought she was going to step away. But her hand reached up, oh so slowly, and she trailed her fingers through the hair above his ear. 'Remind me of that chemistry.' Her voice was low and husky.

He dipped his head to hers. Kissing her

slowly, gently. Conscious they may well have a small pair of eyes on them. Pulling her body next to his, and feeling the tight tension relax as they melded together.

This time, it was him that pulled back. She was breathing hard. 'Seven weeks.'

He nodded. 'Seven weeks.'

'I'm not sure if I'm ready for this,' she admitted. She looked up at him. 'I won't deny the chemistry is still there. But how about we start out as friends? I think that's about all I can promise right now.'

He swallowed hard and nodded.

'I missed you,' she admitted. 'More than you will ever know, and more than I could ever cope with. I just don't know what I can realistically deal with again. Because it's not just you, Lachlan, it's us, and everything that happened between us. Every fight, every damaged moment, every little bit of heartache. I can't just get back the good memories, the bad ones will come too.'

It was clearest thing she'd ever said to him, and it took Lachlan a moment to process. She was right. Their history would always be part of them. For him, it meant they should have fought harder for each other, but he wasn't entirely sure that was what she meant.

Aiden grizzled and Lachlan nudged the crib

back and forward. 'But history—no matter how much we hate it—has made us who we are. We've moved on. We've grown. We can't wipe it away.' He gave a nod of his head. 'Seven weeks, as friends. I think I can manage that.'

His stomach squeezed as he saw Iris give a sigh of relief. She reached into the crib and picked up Aiden, nuzzling him into her neck and rubbing his back.

Iris would have been a great mother. But that was completely the wrong thing to say here, even if watching her actions made him ache inside.

She put her hand on her chest. 'But I still need a bit of space. *We* still need a bit of space.'

'I can live with that.' It was the easiest thing in the world to agree with. Because he wasn't quite sure how he was going to handle this. He still felt as if Iris was keeping her cards close to her chest.

She stood for a few moments, watching him carefully. He could see her start to relax, her shoulders ease and muscles stop clenching. It was almost as if all the anxiety was draining from her body. 'I better get this guy back to his mother,' she said, heading for the door.

Lachlan walked alongside and opened the door for her. 'Friends,' he said in a low voice. 'For seven weeks.'

She nodded, glancing outside to see if anyone was watching them. 'Friends,' she agreed. The corridor was empty.

As she stepped out into the corridor, his arm brushed against hers. 'Friends—' he smiled, then gave her a wink '—with chemistry.'

Then he strode down the corridor before she had a chance to reply.

CHAPTER SIX

IRIS HAD CHANGED three times, much to the amusement of Holly, who sat on her bed, legs crossed, eating chocolate and watching something on her iPad. 'Where are you going, Mum?'

'Out. Not sure where.'

'Then how are you supposed to decide what to wear if you don't know where you're going?' Holly made it sound all so simple. Her long dark hair fell over her face and she was engrossed in the latest episode of a kids' TV series.

Every time she glanced at her daughter Iris's heart swelled. Part of it was circumstances. Background information was limited, but Holly had been given up because neither of her parents had wanted her. Iris didn't know what their circumstances had been, but from the moment she'd met this little girl she'd felt such an affinity to her. Iris knew that Holly had experienced the misfortune of being given up by her parents, then being in a number of foster homes before her placement with Iris when she was four, and Iris still occasionally caught a haunted look on her daughter's face. One that she recognised well. That glimpse of some kind of memory that might not be welcome.

Iris had done her absolute best to ground Holly and fill her life with love and attention. Letting her know she was always safe and secure with her, and that they were family. Holly was, without a doubt, the most important person in the world to her, and her heart ached with the thought that Lachlan still didn't know she existed.

Iris looked around at the black dress, red trousers and white top, and black trousers with a whole host of coloured tops that she was still undecided on.

'Looks like a tornado has swept around this room,' said Holly casually. She was giggling now, because this was an expression that Iris frequently used to describe Holly's room. She laughed too and started hanging things up again. No black dress. No red trousers.

She pulled the black trousers on, along with some flats, and stood staring in the mirror trying to decide what top would be best. Smart? Casual? Or sexy?

No. Definitely not sexy. It was too soon for that. She and Lachlan were treading carefully around each other, almost like a pair of lions stalking prey. She'd had coffee with him a few times. They'd gone back to the library together. All daytime activities. And now, he'd finally suggested they go for dinner. Which was making her nervous—a) because it was a definite night-time activity, and b) because she'd had to arrange a babysitter for Holly and make some excuse for him not to pick her up at home.

The babysitter part had been very easy. Holly was going to stay with her school friend overnight. It was an arrangement that happened frequently between the two families, usually due to the work commitments of both working mums. But this was the first time Iris had asked due to a personal reason. A social reason. And it felt almost like she was taking advantage.

Holly's bag was packed in the corner, waiting for Iris to drop her off on her way into the city centre. She was as excited about the stay, and full of giggles, but was clearly picking up on her mum's nerves.

'That one.' Holly pointed, with a huge grin. 'It's pretty.'

'You're right.' Iris picked up the burgundy top, with a few sparkling sequins scattered across the neckline, and pulled it straight over her head.

Her make-up was done and she shook her hair out, slipped in a pair of earrings and grabbed her leather jacket and bag. She gathered Holly into a huge hug. 'Thank you so much for helping me choose. Now, are you ready?'

Holly was still smiling. She knew her mum was going out with a friend from work, but Iris hadn't mentioned a name. Holly blinked and looked at her mum. 'Is this a girl work friend, or a boy work friend?'

Iris smiled, as she inwardly cringed. She liked that fact that Holly knew no matter where Iris was going, or with whom, she was always completely indecisive about what to wear. She could avoid the truth here, but she didn't want to do that with her daughter.

'It's a boy work friend. He's new to Dublin. But I've worked with him before.' It was clearly a very abbreviated version of life, but it was as much as an seven-year-old should need to know.

Holly stuffed another last-minute toy into her bag. 'What do you think we'll have for breakfast at Katie's tomorrow?'

There it was. Her daughter's favourite subject. It seemed that Iris was sadly lacking in the breakfast department. Katie's mother seemed to dream up things out of nowhere for the girls. Shaped pancakes, flavoured porridge, French toast, home-made waffles. Iris's usual toast and box of cornflakes were never going to make the grade.

The two climbed into Iris's red Mini and five minutes later—after a long conversation about the latest kids' TV show—Holly wrapped her arms around Iris's neck and smothered her in kisses. 'Love you, Mum.'

'Love you, honey. Have a good time and remember you can phone me anytime if you want to.' Holly grinned and then skipped up the stairs in Katie's house with her friend.

Iris's heart gave a little pang as she thanked Katie's mum and said goodbye. Adopting Holly was, without a doubt, the best thing she'd ever done. That settled like a weight around her shoulders. She still hadn't told Lachlan about her daughter. They were treading so carefully around each other right now and she was afraid to rock the boat.

The answer was simple, really; she just had to gather her courage and tell him. But she wasn't quite sure how he would react to the news. When he'd mentioned adoption to her in the past, and she'd no, he'd dropped it, so easily. He hadn't pried. He hadn't pushed, and it made her wonder if he'd really only ever been fixed on having children of his own. Would he even be interested in Holly? And if he wasn't, how would that make her, Iris, feel? No, she really needed to get a better sense of things first.

Timing was everything, she told herself. But each day that passed seemed like another opportunity lost. As friends, they were getting closer. Every time they were together she could feel the barriers that had been built between them gradually breaking down, little by little. The kiss had certainly helped. At least, it had certainly given her a few sleepless nights.

She shivered, remembering it in delight as she pulled into a car park in the city. She'd made an excuse for meeting like this, and quickly checked her make-up before climbing out of the car.

Lachlan was leaning against his own car, smiling at her. She walked over to meet him. 'Well, are you going to tell me where we're going?'

It was a beautiful mild evening. The streets were busy with people casually walking around. 'I'm going to surprise you,' he said as he held out his hand to her.

She hesitated for the briefest of seconds, then reached and slid her hand into his. Was this a step too far for friends? But the feel of his hand encompassing hers made her smile all over again. They'd always held hands. Never while they were working. But all the time in their previous daily lives. This felt natural. It felt good. And she wanted to capture some of those moments again.

They started walking through the streets, stopping to look in the window of a bookshop, and then again at an antique shop. He gave her a sideways glance.

'What?' she asked, checking her appearance in a nearby window—had she smudged something?

'You've got your hair down. It's lovely. You always have it up at work.'

She'd forgotten she'd left her hair down and gave it an unconscious shake. Her blonde hair had always fallen in natural waves. Products and styling were not required.

Lachlan had always loved it.

Her free hand came up and twisted a lock around her finger. 'Yeah, I don't wear it down much these days. Too busy. Too much time spent at work.'

'You need to get out more. Enjoy yourself.' There was a hint of something in his eyes. She liked it. It sparked something down deep inside her, like a slow burning flame.

'Hungry?' he asked.

'Absolutely. If you don't tell me where we're

going soon, I'm going to raid the nearest bar, and order twenty-five bags of crisps.'

He laughed. 'Oh, we can't have that.' He gave a nod to the other end of the street. 'It's just along here.'

She tilted her head, trying to see any of the approaching signs, but her vision wasn't quite that good. It took her a few moments to realise where they were going. 'Here?' she asked, her eyebrows rising.

Lachlan nodded and gestured for her to enter the well-known hotel. Iris couldn't help but smile as they walked through the foyer and took the lift to the top floor. The restaurant in this hotel was extremely popular. It had floor-to-ceiling windows all the way around, a large circular bar in the middle and breathtaking views of Dublin city and the mountains.

The wooden décor was cool and funky, and there were booths at the windows, offering a little privacy, along with the spectacular scenery. Iris couldn't stop smiling as they were shown to their seats. 'I've always wanted to come here.'

'You haven't been before?'

She shook her head. 'I was supposed to come here once, for a colleague's leaving do, but I ended up having to cover that night and couldn't come. I was livid,' she admitted as the waiter handed over their menus. 'I'd already picked what I wanted on the menu that night.'

He shook his head. 'Well, I'm glad I've brought you somewhere that you haven't experienced yet.'

They ordered drinks and Iris leaned back into her comfortable seat and looked out over the city and mountains. 'It really is a great view,' she sighed. 'People tell you about it, and you can see it from the gallery photos on the website.' She sucked in a breath. 'But actually *being* here, and seeing it for yourself, is entirely different.'

She looked across the table at him. Lachlan always managed to look good no matter what he wore. His black polo shirt was casual, but smart, his hair was at the perfect stage where it was still short, but had just enough hint of his natural curl. There were a few tiny strands of grey around his temples, but it was always the deep brown eyes that got her.

There was so much behind them, so much depth. Sometimes she thought she could read his whole mind by just looking into those eyes. As she glanced at the menu his hand crept across the table and his fingers intertwined with hers.

She gave a deep sigh and looked back him, struck by the fact that Lachlan hadn't even realised that he'd done it. Eight years on, and they could still fit back into their old loving habits. And instead of making her panic about moving too fast, it gave her the greatest sensation of comfort. Love. Eternal love, that she'd always thought she would never find again.

No one had ever made her feel the way Lachlan had done. No one had ever set her on fire like he did, engaged her mind and her body. Understood her in ways she didn't understand herself. In the end, none of it had helped keep them together—and she pushed that last thought out of her head because this night she just wanted to remember the good.

The waiter appeared to deliver their drinks and take their order and Iris didn't hesitate. 'Can I have the roast pepper, paprika and sweet potato soup, followed by the pan-fried salmon, please?'

Lachlan gave her a nod of approval. 'I'll have the same,' he said, handing back his menu.

'Don't you want the steak?' she asked in surprise as she took a long drink of chilled rosé wine.

He shook his head. 'After eating it for around five years straight I realised I had to change my eating habits.'

She lifted her glass to him. 'You're learning

to widen your eating habits?' It was something she'd gently chided him about regularly.

'Oh, there's lots I've learned,' he teased.

She glanced around. 'So, how did you know about this place?'

He smiled widely. 'I asked my local expert where the best place for a first date would be.'

First date. The words sent a shiver down her spine. 'This is a first date?'

'I think so.' He looked at her curiously. 'Why? What would you call it?'

She wrinkled her brow. 'I'm not sure, a reunion?' She shook her head. 'No, that doesn't seem right. A blast from the past?' She shook her head again. 'No, a drink between friends?' None of the terms seemed to fit them.

Lachlan took a drink of his beer. 'No, this is *definitely* a first date. And that's how we will treat this. Two new people, out for dinner—' he gave her a wink '—dressed to impress, in a beautiful setting, with a lot of promise in the air.'

She couldn't help the mischievous words. 'You think there's promise in the air? Well, that means you'll have to impress.' She raised her eyebrows. 'Think you've got the skills?'

He raised his bottle of beer to her. 'I guess we'll find out.'

Tingles darted down her spine. This is what

she'd wanted. This is what she'd missed. That chat. That banter. The playful promise of what might come next. It had been so long. Sure, she'd dated. Sometimes for a few months at a time.

But nothing had replicated the relationship she'd had with Lachlan. And now, in this beautiful restaurant, with the three-hundred-and-sixty-degree views around them, she was drinking in the view of the man she'd loved so long ago.

His hint of curls, thoughtful brown eyes, the tiny wrinkles around the edges of both his eyes and his lips. The broad shoulders, and wide chest. The way when he was next to her, his large stance made her feel protected, shielded from the world. She could have done with that over the last eight years.

'I'm so sorry,' she blurted out.

He blinked and froze. 'For what?'

The waiter appeared and sat down their soup. Iris stared at it for a few moments as she tried to find the words. 'For…just…everything.'

She didn't look back up. It was all so overwhelming. Being here with Lachlan was something she'd wanted to be fun. But she had to say something out loud—about their past, their history and their break-up. They'd never really had that final conversation. They'd just packed up as agreed and gone their separate ways. It had all been so civilised, even though they'd both been tremendously sad.

Iris had been utterly heartbroken. But she'd never wanted to admit it to herself when she'd been the one to push for them to part.

Lachlan's hand reached back across the table and touched hers. 'I know,' he said quietly. The buzz up her arm was instant. 'And so am I.'

That was just like him. He didn't take the opportunity to apportion blame and lay it at her door. Another reason he'd always had her heart.

'Eat your dinner,' he said in a joking tone, clearly trying to lighten the mood. 'Don't get bogged down by the past tonight. Let's just enjoy ourselves in the here and now. There's plenty of time for the other stuff later. Deal?'

She looked up and he raised his bottle of beer. It was as though the wave of guilt and regret that had flooded over her just ebbed away again. He'd given her permission not to linger on past regrets. And for tonight? She could do that.

She clinked her wine glass against his. 'Done.' She picked up the spoon and tasted her soup. Her taste buds exploded. It was delicious. His leg brushed against hers under the table and she smiled as another kind of zing shot through her. This night had started with hand-holding and she had a deep suspicion she knew where it might go.

Three hours passed in a flash. The wine, beer and food flowed. The lights outside grew dimmer and by the time the waiter had cleared their plates away the sky was a mixed range of oranges, purples and dark blues.

'Coffee?'

'Irish,' she said promptly.

'Hmm…' said Lachlan as he watched her, nodding to the waiter. 'Two Irish coffees, please.'

'I'll need to get a taxi,' she sighed, leaning back against the padded booth.

'*We'll* need to get a taxi,' Lachlan corrected.

'A late-night walk through the city might be nice. Especially at sunset.'

Lachlan looked out at the spectacular evening colours. 'Next time we should take a drive out to the mountains. Watch the sunset from there.'

'Next time?' She knew that her voice sounded hopeful, but she wasn't ashamed to admit it.

'Why wouldn't there be a next time,' said Lachlan, his voice casual. Part of that annoyed her, and part of her was amused by it. Was he really so relaxed about what was happening between them again? Every time his leg brushed against hers, or he touched her hand, she felt the sparks in the air between them.

She let herself drink in the warmth those words spread through her body, pushing aside the little voice in her head that warned her there were still some things she needed to be honest about with Lachlan.

She was sure there was just as much she didn't know about him. He'd been distinctly sketchy about the last eight years—and, for now, that was fine. She wasn't ready to hear about anyone else he might have loved in her place. She knew no one had featured in his place in her life, but *he* didn't know that, just like he didn't know about the decision she'd taken around parenthood. And she would tell him. Soon.

It wasn't like there hadn't been dates before. Holly had only ever met two men that Iris had dated, and she'd cut both relationships short when she'd realised she'd never consider anything long term with either of them.

But now?

She'd thought for ever would be Lachlan Brodie. And it hadn't been. The voice in the back of her head kept reminding her he was here on a temporary basis and he already had another job waiting for him. If this amounted to anything, it would be short, and maybe a little bittersweet.

Yet a fire burned deep inside her. The chemistry between them still seemed so strong. Part of her longed to push forward, to see if they still connected in the bedroom the way that they previously had.

The coffee laced with whisky warmed her even more. And when the bill had been settled and they started walking the darker streets, it was easy to let Lachlan slip his arm around her shoulders and for her to lean her head against him and slip one hand against his flat stomach.

Their pace was slower, both sedated by the good food and alcohol. Iris guided them to the nearest taxi rank. She turned to face him and he said the magic words. 'Would you like to come and see my cottage?'

She knew the taxi ride to her house would be quicker. But her house showed signs everywhere of the fact she had a daughter. Even though Holly was staying with a friend tonight, she couldn't take him to her house without being honest with him—whether Holly was there or not.

She slid her arms around his waist. 'I'd love to see your cottage.' And the truth was, she did want to see it. He clearly loved his temporary accommodation, as he mentioned it frequently.

She was curious about how much of himself he had imprinted on the place.

A taxi drew forward and Lachlan opened the door for her, giving the driver the address as he climbed in.

Around twenty minutes later he signalled the driver to drop them at the bottom of a well-lit lane and paid the fare.

Iris was already smiling as he took her hand and led her towards the grey brick cottage with a slightly wonky-looking roof. The lane was wide enough for cars and had several lights along it. Lachlan's cottage was around halfway along and had a dark blue door.

He drew out his keys and opened the door. She was instantly hit by the rush of warmth against the cooler night air.

She stepped inside and looked around. The door led straight into the main room that had two double squishy sofas, a central coffee table, a side table and large fireplace. One window looked out onto the lane, and the other looked back over the countryside.

She walked over to the back window immediately, then took a few moments to finger the dark red checked curtains. They just looked so right. The inside stone window ledge was wide enough to sit on and she turned back around and looked at the rest of the room. The sofas were dark green, and had red cushions to match the curtains, and there was a thick red rectangular rug under the coffee table stretching out across the room.

'Wow,' she said, realising the deep scent she was smelling came from the bowl of old-fashioned potpourri on the wooden sideboard.

She held out her hands. 'This place is just so…cottagey!' she finished because there was just no other word that fitted.

Lachlan let out a deep throaty laugh as he locked the front door. His head was only a few inches underneath the ceiling height of the room. But he was obviously used to it, because he didn't duck or stoop. 'Of course it is. Why do you think I love it so much?'

Iris kicked off her shoes, sat down on one of the sofas and tucked her legs under her. This place was instantly comfortable.

'Oh, no, you don't,' said Lachlan. 'You've not had the full tour.'

'I'm getting a tour?' she asked.

'Of course. It's your first visit. Isn't that an unwritten tradition?'

Iris sighed and pushed herself off the sofa, moving over to his side and nudging him with her hip. 'Go on, then, give me the tour.'

They stepped into the kitchen and she was impressed by the large traditional cast-iron stove, and the pale green kitchen around them. Anywhere else it might have looked quite twee, but here, it was just perfect.

'Do you want something to drink? Tea? Coffee? Wine?'

'You have wine?'

He nodded and pulled a bottle of white from the fridge and two glasses from one of the kitchen cupboards. Her foot caught something on the floor. Two dog bowls. 'I thought the dog was Maeve's?'

Lachlan gave a guilty smile. 'Yes, he is. But he spends quite a bit of time around here. I thought it made sense to get him some things.'

'You realise he's playing you, don't you? Should we call him two-dinners Scout?'

Lachlan handed her a glass of wine. 'Oh, one hundred per cent he plays me, but I've not told Maeve about the dog bowls. I figure, what happens between us boys, stays between us boys.'

She shook her head as he led her back out to the main room and showed her the obviously repurposed bathroom, alongside a smaller room that Lachlan was using as a study, and finally, he pushed open a large oak door to reveal his bedroom.

Iris wasn't shy. She stepped inside and sat on the edge of the white uncovered duvet. 'This is bigger than I expected.'

around her body and rested on her
ch. Her bare stomach.

ery part of her tensed. It was an automatic
x as her brain finally reminded her where
was. The clothes lying scattered at the bot-
m of the bed told the story of their evening.
he couldn't even see her bra and had no idea
where it had ended up.

Last night had been scary, but also very,
very natural. Two people who had known
each other intimately before, coming together
with no hesitation. The familiarity had given
them both confidence. The memories of each
other remained, but being a few years older had
made Iris appreciate just how great their mutual chemistry was. She'd never experienced
pleasure in bed with anyone like she had with
Lachlan.

She'd actually begun to tell herself that she'd
imagined it. It couldn't quite have been as good
as she'd remembered, and that she might have
been overplaying it in her memories.

But no. Last night had heightened and rein-
forced every memory she'd ever had. Her skin
still tingled at the mere thought. It was simple.
Lachlan had ruined her for any other man.

'Hey,' the soft voice murmured in her ear.
'What are you doing awake so early?'

Lachlan nodded. 'This room and the room at
the side were a later extension of the cottage.
The bathroom was doubled in size then too.'

'So, if all this was taken off, that was the
original size?'

'Apparently. Maeve said she's got old papers
that stated a family of eight used to live in here.'

Iris immediately drew her arms in as if she
were being squished. 'Eight? That must have
been a tight squeeze.' Her hand brushed over
the duvet cover and she looked around again.
There was a large armchair next to the back
window in the room. She could see one of
Lachlan's jackets, a few pairs of shoes and a
couple of books perched on the deep window-
sill. At the other side of the room was a dark
wood wardrobe, and she could see what she'd
once called his 'doctor's bag.' It was brown
leather, old and battered. Not like the modern
lightweight waterproof bags that were available now.

'I see you've still got your old friend,' she
murmured, taking a sip of her wine.

He gave a nod of acknowledgement, and
she watched as the memories flitted across his
eyes. 'Stethoscope, stitches, scalpel, aspirin,
blood pressure monitor, pocket airway mask,
finger oximeter and glucometer. A few other
bandages and drugs.'

'You still take it with you?' Her voice echoed with nostalgia for Lachlan and the fact he'd used to throw the bag in the boot of whatever car he was travelling in, no matter what the purpose of his journey.

'Of course I do. Never know what you might need in an emergency situation.'

'I bet it could tell a few tales.'

'Oh, it absolutely could.' He was leaning against the door jamb. He'd only taken a few sips of his wine.

Iris looked at him. The guy that even after all these years, one glimpse of, set her heart racing. It seemed ridiculous that one person could still do that to another, with absolutely no contact, after all this time.

But she couldn't ignore the fact, and she absolutely didn't want to.

'What?' He gave her a soft grin. Darn it, still sexy.

She gave up any pretence of resistance. 'I'm just wondering, how it is possible, that after eight years apart, you still make my heart beat just as quickly as ever.'

His lips turned upwards even further. It was almost like a licence for him to move. He took a few steps towards her, stopping midway between the door and the bed. 'Pheromones,' he said in a low, deep voice.

tory. And who knows what ⌐

She stood up and took a ste Her skin tingled to reach out an But she wanted to know it wasn't ju wanted to know that he felt exactly way she did.

'Is it the same for you?' she whispered.

He gave her a blazing look. 'It is.'

It was all she needed to hear right now.

His voice was husky. 'Are you going to stay the night?'

Of course. Holly was safe with someone else. The night was hers to do what she wanted with.

And she knew exactly what she wanted to do with it.

She stepped forward and put her hand to his face. 'I think I could be persuaded.' She smiled.

He dipped his mouth towards hers. And persuaded her.

Iris woke as the early morning sun hit her face. Pure and utter comfort. That was her first thought. The second was a bit more alarming. She was in that hazy spot, where the brain takes a few moments to orientate to time and place. The heat from the bed wasn't coming from the covers, it was coming from the warm body tucked in behind hers. A large arm was

She blinked and smiled, turning around to face him. 'What time is it?' she asked sleepily.

'Five o'clock. Guess I forgot to close the curtains.'

She kept smiling. 'I think you were distracted.'

He dropped a kiss on her lips. 'I think I was.'

He laughed. 'Did that really happen, or was something in the wine last night and I just hallucinated the most spectacular dream of my life?'

She reached up and touched the edge of his cheek. 'It happened,' she agreed, her stomach turning over. After the passionately intimate night they'd just spent together, she knew she had to be honest with him. She had to take the bulk of the blame for their split, and she had to let him know exactly how she'd moved on. She had to tell him about Holly.

'Lachlan,' she said quietly.

His eyes opened. He'd heard the wary tone in her voice. 'What's wrong?' His hand was stroking gently up and down her back.

'I have to tell you something.'

'You can tell me anything, Iris,' he said, with a quiet reassurance that made her more nervous than ever.

She kept her hand on his cheek. It anchored her. But as she spoke she closed her eyes, because it made her more comfortable. 'You know you mentioned adoption to me in the past. And I told you no.'

She felt his body stiffen a little next to hers. Even though she wasn't watching, she knew he would be looking at her right now. 'I know you were adopted yourself. I respected your decision to say no.'

She swallowed awkwardly, wishing he'd said a bit more back then.

'Being adopted wasn't a fairy-tale experience for me,' she said quickly.

His hand continued to stroke up and down her back, as if he were doing it now to offer comfort. 'Tell me about it.'

'I don't have a lot of early memories. I have to assume I was happy initially. My memories really start with my mum telling me she was having a baby of her own.'

'Okay.' It was a statement, but he made it sound more like a question.

'I remember her stomach getting bigger. I must have been around six then. I learned later that they'd desperately wanted a baby of their own, it hadn't happened, and then after they'd had me for a few years, it just happened naturally.' She opened her eyes now. 'The way that everyone tells us that story.'

Lachlan gave a slow nod. They'd had multiple friends offer similar stories when they'd been on their own fertility journey. 'Stop trying' had been a favourite recommendation. But friends often didn't realise how much their own words and stories could hurt.

'So, what happened?' he coaxed.

Iris pressed her lips together for a second, trying to stop the tears forming. But they were there. Telling the story made it all so real and painful again.

'My mum was completely distracted during her pregnancy, totally focused on what was happening to her. Suddenly, I was too loud. Too demanding. I had too many activities. I wanted too much of her time. In the end, my parents stopped my dance lessons and my swimming lessons, telling me they would be too busy to take me when the baby came along. It was like as soon as they knew they were having a baby of their own, I became nothing more than an unwelcome inconvenience to them.'

'Iris, that's terrible.' A deep furrow creased his brow.

She shrugged. 'It is. But that was my life from then on. My sister was born, and it seemed like I couldn't have a second of their time. They didn't celebrate my successes. When I did well at school, it was like they didn't even care. My sister was always the centre of attention. And because there were six years between us, as the years passed, I did what most kids would probably do. I acted out. I misbehaved. I got into trouble. Anything really to get some kind of attention from them, but it just made every-thing worse.' Tears were falling now. 'It took a teacher, who recognised what was going on and helped me realise the opportunities I could let slip away, to focus on myself and my studies again. Mrs Kelly helped me with my applica-tion for medical school; she made it possible for me to attend the after-school lessons by drop-ping me home afterwards. Both of my parents had said they couldn't possibly pick me up, and the school bus service had always finished by that time. It felt as if she were the only adult that ever noticed me.'

Lachlan brushed a tear away from her cheek. 'That's awful. I want to kill them. How dare they treat you like that? What kind of adults do that? I always wondered why they didn't come to our wedding. You said it was because they were in Australia, but I still thought it was strange they didn't even phone or send a message.'

Iris shook her head. 'I don't think they would have come even if they had been in this coun-try.' She moved her hand from his cheek and pressed it against her chest. 'They never made me feel loved. I never felt wanted. I always felt as if I just shouldn't be there. And when you suggested adoption to me as a possible way forward for us…'

She let the words tail off.

She didn't want to have to spell it out for him. She wanted to move on. She wanted to tell him that she'd finally healed. She wanted to tell him about Holly now.

But Lachlan never gave her the chance.

He sat up quickly, unwrapping himself from around Iris so he could look at her clearly, without mounds of pillows and blankets in the way. His brain was trying to piece together everything she'd just revealed about herself.

Had he ever actually known Iris at all?

'Why didn't you tell me all this before?' was all that he could start with.

Iris looked hurt he'd pulled away, and she pushed herself up too and sat back against the pillows. 'Because I was young. I was in love. My husband wanted a family. *I* wanted a family. And when it didn't happen—' she held up her hands '—it seemed that everything just fell apart.'

Lachlan couldn't help what he was sure was a look of disbelief on his face. He still couldn't find the right place to start. 'This was important information, Iris. I was your husband. This was the kind of stuff you should have told me. Don't you think I could see how much you were falling apart? Why didn't you trust me enough to tell me about your childhood? You knew that I loved you. I would have done anything for you, Iris. But you didn't tell me any of this, which would have helped me understand you better, and you just kept pushing me further and further away.'

Iris looked hurt but she nodded. Her pale blue eyes met his and her voice trembled. 'But how do you tell the first person who actually loves you in the universe that no one else thought you worthy of love before? What if I tell you something like that, and you decide I'm not worthy of love either?'

It felt like a slap in the face. He'd noticed her change in tense. She'd changed from the past tense, to the present. Her words cut him to the bone—the fact this his wife had actually *felt* like that and hadn't told him. Clearly still felt like it. Just how much damage had her parents done—and did they even know, or care?

Now he realised what drove her so hard to wanting children of her own, and what had inevitably led to her falling apart after she'd failed to conceive.

He kept his voice low. His own emotions

had to be contained, because he could see how much those words had cost her.

'These were things you should have told me—or I feel as if I should have just known or realised. I thought we knew all about each other, Iris. I spilled my guts to you about everything. Our connection felt so real, so in tune.' He swallowed. 'But I obviously didn't give you the security that you needed. And I'm sorry, because I thought I had. I thought our marriage started out somewhere close to perfect—' he gave a sorry excuse for a laugh '—but I was clearly blind. Our marriage was nowhere near as healthy as I thought. If it had been, you would have felt safe opening up to me. We might have had a chance to work through all this if you'd been able to talk to me.'

Her fingers reached over and stroked the back of his hand. 'If only we could turn back time.' She shook her head. 'I wish I could have had the knowledge and experience I have now, back then. I was desperate to have a perfect life. But it wasn't just us that was affected, Lachlan, it was everything in my life. I struggled to open up to people because of the constant fear of rejection. I understand that now.' She gave a half-hearted smile. 'A good few years in therapy helped me unpick all that.' She sighed. 'If I could turn back time for us, I would wait.'

He frowned. 'Wait? You mean, not get married?' He was surprised how much that hurt.

But Iris shook her head. 'No,' she said sadly. 'I would always have married you.' And those words gave him a little comfort, as she continued. 'But I wouldn't have been in such a rush to start a family. To go through everything that we did. If we'd taken a bit more time together, before we got swept away with the idea of creating a perfect family, then I think we might have discovered each other a bit more. Had a little more resilience for what lay ahead of us.'

Lachlan's heart squeezed. It struck him that he still knew barely more about Iris now than he did back then. What other things might he not know about her? They'd clearly moved too fast yet again, carried away by the incredible chemistry that still existed between them.

His alarm sounded loudly, making them both jump. Iris glanced at the clock. 'Darn it. I need to get home and get a change of clothes before heading to work.'

She swung her legs out of the bed and started grabbing last night's clothes. 'The cars,' he groaned. 'They're both back in the city centre. I'll call us a cab.'

He made the call first, then quickly washed and dressed for work. He would be able to drive straight to work once he picked up his car. Iris, however, would need to make a journey home first. He wrinkled his nose. 'Do you want me to go and ask Maeve if she has anything she can lend you?' He looked down at her dress trousers and sequined top.

The air was weighted with sadness. Something had changed. The conversation had dragged up parts of the past they'd both pushed aside for a while. And it was clear they were both aware of it.

Iris shook her head. 'Then she would tease you mercilessly. Some secrets should be kept.'

Their eyes met and he saw Iris flinch. She'd only been talking about their night together, but the words just seemed ill-timed in light of their previous conversation. The taxi beeped outside the door and she seemed only too relieved to open it.

'Let's go,' she said, and Lachlan nodded, locking the door behind them slowly, his brain still whirring—not entirely sure what might come next.

CHAPTER SEVEN

IRIS WAS FEELING kind of melancholy. She was even more confused than ever. Lachlan had been distant for the last week. She kept going over in her head how hurt and disappointed he'd been after she'd told him about her past, that she'd not confided in him before. How on earth would he take the news about Holly, because now, more than ever, she felt as if she had to tell him.

He needed to know. He deserved to know. And maybe she was panicking about nothing. It could be that Lachlan would have no reaction to the fact she'd adopted a child on her own. It was her right, of course.

But part of her was fearful. Their night together had been wonderful, and she couldn't get that chemistry and connection out of her head. She'd already thought he might have ruined her for any other man, and now she was sure. What they had between them was special. It seemed that there was more at stake than ever.

So, she really, really needed to have the conversation about Holly. He needed to know all her truths. It no longer mattered to her that he only had a few weeks left of a three-month contract. No matter where he was going in this world, she wanted him to know that Holly existed. She had no idea what that might mean for them. But if she was only ever going to have this kind of connection with one man, then she needed to be honest with him. Could there ever be a future for her and Lachlan? She didn't know. She might spend the rest of her life as a single mum with Holly. If that happened, she would be happy. She would. But she also had to be true to herself and her feelings for Lachlan.

Iris walked through the unit. It was busy today. A typical Saturday afternoon, building up to likely a busy Saturday night.

She scanned the board. Fergus was working, alongside Ryan, Joan and Lachlan. With those senior staff, she expected everything to be under control.

Joan was triaging, rapidly assessing all patients. Ryan was looking after someone in Resus, and Fergus seemed to be co-ordinating the floor.

'Have you seen Lachlan?'

Fergus nodded. 'He's in bay four with a sick kid. Running a few tests. It looked just like some regular virus, but Lachlan's worried.'

Iris nodded and walked over to the nurses' station, picking up a tablet and having a quick scan of what was recorded.

She made her way to the bay and pulled back the curtains. 'Good afternoon,' she said to the man at the side. 'I'm Dr Conway. Just in to see how your little boy is doing.'

Lachlan looked up and lifted his stethoscope from the child's chest. He scribbled a few notes and handed them to her.

Temperature for last few days. Rash. Swollen lymph nodes. It could literally be any sick child in the world.

Children often came in, with parents in near tears with worry, only for them to perk up a few hours later as if they hadn't been sick at all. She'd witnessed it herself with Holly. The resilience of children was never to be underestimated—alongside the ability for the parent to feel like a panicking fool. Even though she was a doctor, Iris had worn that badge herself, more than once.

But this little guy looked exhausted. His chest was bare, and he was curled up on his side.

Lachlan was talking quietly to the little boy.

'Here, Fletch, I'm just going to take a look in your throat. Can you open your mouth for me?'

The little boy obliged, and Iris wondered if he had some kind of tonsilitis. But Lachlan then sat down in a chair next to a man who she presumed was the dad, and took one of Fletch's hands. He took a few moments, and then stood and lifted the hospital blanket and glanced down at Fletch's feet. Something inside her brain switched on. Lachlan gave her a nod, as if he'd realised she would catch on to what he was thinking.

He turned to the dad. 'Alan, you were absolutely right to bring Fletch in. I think there's something a little more wrong with him than just a virus, but the first thing I'm going to say to you is that this will be entirely treatable.'

Iris moved closer. Now, she could see the cracks at the sides of Fletch's lips, his puffy eyes and how swollen his fingers were, just like his toes. Classic signs, that could on occasion be missed by a less skilled physician.

'I'm almost sure that Fletch has something called Kawasaki disease. It generally affects kids under five, and Fletch has all the signs. A temperature for more than a few days, a rash, the cracks around his lips and his swollen fingers and toes. He might also develop some peeling skin from the palms of his hands and feet.' He put his hand on the sleeping little boy. 'It's important this disease is picked up quickly and treated. So, we'll admit him to Paediatrics and start him on some immunoglobulin. The best way to get the medicine into him is through a drip, so I'll have to put something in his arm. We also have to give him a medicine we don't normally give kids. You'll have heard of it—aspirin.'

Alan wrinkled his brow. 'The health visitor said we're not allowed to give him that until he's twelve. He's only three.'

Lachlan nodded. Iris couldn't help but admire how good he was being with this dad and this little boy. He had a gentle manner, but was also very clear when explaining things. She would expect any doctor to be like this. But watching Lachlan was making her heart squeeze.

'He is. And this is one of the only occasions we'd use this medicine. It's likely he'll need to take it for a few weeks.' Lachlan stood up and held his hand out to Alan, shaking it in a reassuring manner. 'Let me go and talk to my colleagues in Paediatrics, they'll come down and see you straight away. I'm going to go and get some cream to numb Fletch's skin so he won't feel the needle when we put it in.'

Iris followed him as they walked back to the

nursing station. 'Checking up on me?' he asked. She knew he was joking but his expression was serious. It was clear he was worried about the little boy.

'Good catch,' she said. 'Someone else might have missed it.'

He shrugged. 'Let's just say I have a vested interest in these things. The paediatrician had been notified to come down, but we had a baby with suspected meningitis earlier, so I suspect they are still dealing with that case. I'll give them a phone.'

Iris was stuck on the first part of the sentence. 'What do you mean you've got a vested interest?'

He paused as he picked up the phone. 'I'll explain later.'

She held her tongue and let him do his job. Kawasaki syndrome could lead to heart conditions in children. Fletch would need to be monitored for the next few years. She'd never seen a case herself, but knew that not all children had the specific symptoms, and sometimes things were missed. The fact that Lachlan had caught this on first examination was impressive.

She treated a few patients herself while waiting for him to finish, then joined him in the coffee lounge.

He had a strange look on his face when she sat down next to him. 'Are you okay?'

He gave a tight-lipped nod, then shook his head and leaned forward, resting his arms on his legs. 'Just brought back some difficult memories for me.'

She was careful now, conscious there was a whole eight years she knew very little about, and even more aware that she still had important things to share with him too. 'Okay, tell me.'

He sighed. 'We haven't told each other much about the last few years. But I'm sure you'll have lived your life, just like I have.'

She gave a nod, her chest tight. She had a horrible feeling she wouldn't like what came next.

'I met someone. Her name was Lorraine and we were good friends, comfortable around each other. We decided to get out of the city and bought a house in the countryside to make a few changes to our lives.'

'You didn't work in A&E any more?'

He gave a short laugh. 'You'll hate this, but I did my GP training. Looking back, it wasn't really for me. But it suited me at the time. It suited us.'

She was astonished. Lachlan had always liked being in the thick of the action, much like she did. He had mentioned doing something else, but he hadn't given much away. But it was the other words he'd said that she was fixating on. Lorraine. Every part of her had an instant irrational dislike to whoever this person was. You didn't buy a house and change your whole life for someone who was just a good friend.

'So, what happened?' Her voice felt a bit wobbly.

He took a deep breath. 'Lorraine was a doctor, just like us. She picked up a virus—like we all have, a million times over. But this virus became viral cardiomyopathy. She became sick very, very quickly. She ended up on the heart transplant list but never managed to get one.' He ran his hand through his hair. 'The truth was, she probably would never have survived the surgery. Her consultant was astonished at the rate of her disease progression. It was all just so quick.'

Iris was shocked. She didn't know quite what she'd expected to hear, but it certainly wasn't that.

'So, your partner died?'

He nodded and gave her a sad smile.

'I'm sorry, Lachlan. That must have been so hard on you.'

'It was,' he acknowledged. 'And today might have been a different disease, but we know what can happen if Kawasaki syndrome goes undetected and the damage it can do to hearts.'

'How long has it been since she passed away?'

She was feeling utterly selfish. She'd been so wrapped up in her own secrets, she hadn't really considered Lachlan's. He hadn't used the word *love* when talking about Lorraine. But she had to assume it had been there.

'Over a year since she died.' He sighed. 'And it was only a few months ago that I realised I wasn't really living any more. I didn't enjoy my job. I didn't enjoy my life. I needed a new place, and a chance...' His voice tailed off and he didn't finish.

Iris wanted to fill in the space. There were so many ways she could finish that sentence: a chance to start again, to look for love, to rekindle a romance?

Or maybe she was being too hopeful. It could be: a chance to get away from everything, to forget about the past—which would put a whole other slant on things.

So many things were racing through her brain as she thought about the words he'd just used to describe Lorraine. Good friends. Comfortable around each other. But had he loved the calm, sensible-sounding Lorraine more than he was revealing after the turmoil and trauma of their marriage? All of sudden she felt on even more shaky ground.

'A chance to what?' She couldn't let her mind keep filling in the blanks.

He held both hands upwards. 'A chance to do this again. A chance to get a fire in my belly for my working life again.'

He reached out and took her hand with a sigh. 'It's also given me the chance to see you again.' His deep brown eyes looked at her. 'I wanted to apologise. I've spent the last week thinking about it, and I know how hard it was for you to tell me about your childhood. I'm sorry I didn't react the way I should have. It should never have been about me. It should always just have been about you. I felt as if I'd let you down because you didn't feel you could trust me with this before.' He squeezed her hand. 'And I know you probably needed space and time away from me to do that. I just wish things could have been different for us.'

For the first time in a week she felt bold enough to ask a question out loud. 'So, what about now? Are you glad that you came to Dublin? Are you glad that we've met again?'

Maybe it wasn't appropriate to ask that question now. But Iris felt as if Lachlan had just pulled the carpet out from beneath her feet. She'd no idea he'd lost a partner relatively recently. And all of a sudden she wondered if the connection she'd relived during their night together had just been pure fantasy.

Lachlan gave a small laugh and squeezed her hand. 'You were a surprise. A blessing almost. Although I'll never get over the shock of looking up and seeing you standing there.'

'I'll never get over the horror of hearing you tell me my department was a mess.'

He shook his head. 'Not my finest moment. In my defence, I was pretty stunned.'

His thumb started making little circles on the inside of her palm. It gave her confidence to ask another question.

'So... Lorraine?'

Lachlan looked at her. She could see the softness around his eyes.

'What about her?'

'Were you married? Engaged?'

He shook his head. 'No. Nothing like that.'

'But you bought a house together. Moved to the country together. You must have loved her.'

'I did,' he said without hesitation, and Iris found her breath catching in the back of her throat. 'Lorraine was a good person. She'd had a previous relationship that hadn't worked out. She'd been hurt—like I was.'

The hairs pricked on the back of Iris's neck.

He was talking about *them*. She shifted uncomfortably on the chair.

Lachlan kept talking. It was so matter-of-fact. 'Lorraine was easy. She was comfortable to be around. We didn't fight or argue. If I had a bad day at work, we could come home and talk about it. If I came home and wanted to tramp about the hills for a few hours, she never minded.' He lowered his eyes. 'I cared about her a lot. I loved her in the way that you love a good friend. We were companions more than anything. Sure, at times, things were physical between us, but we didn't have huge plans for the future. We never talked about marriage or a family. I think she very much felt the same way I did. Happy to have someone to share things with and be comfortable around.'

Iris was struggling to get her head around this. She understood the words, but not the emotions. She'd never had that kind of relationship before.

But Lachlan wasn't finished. 'But when she was diagnosed and became sick, it all got too real. Lorraine was terrified. It was as if, right from the beginning, she understood how ill she was, and how things would go. She was calm but scared. I spent most nights just holding her. She cried for all the things she wasn't going to get to do, and she used to get really upset when I tried to placate her and say that things would be fine.'

'But that's understandable. I get it. She must have felt as though her life was being stolen from her. The unfairness of the disease is horrible.'

'But I was overwhelmed by how much it made me realise what Lorraine meant to me.' Iris's insides twisted. She wasn't sure she liked this, but now she'd asked the question, Lachlan couldn't seem to stop talking.

'At that point, she was my best friend. I hated she was sick. I hated that she hadn't got what she wanted out of this life. I did everything for her. Helped her into the shower. Sometimes helped her get changed. Washed her hair. Made the dinners. And she hated being helpless as much as I hated seeing my friend suffer. It was so unfair. In the meantime, I was still working as a GP, and supporting other families that were in similar positions to me—nursing a family member with a terminal condition. I always thought I understood and got it, but I realised then that I hadn't. It had all been assumptions and sympathy on my part. Then I understood not being able to sleep at night and not really being able to work out why. I understood why I could reach the end of the day, realise I hadn't eaten a thing all day and wonder why I hadn't been hungry. It all made sense to me. And I started looking at those people differently, talking to them more. Calling them into the surgery to ask them how they were doing, instead of waiting for them to appear with symptoms.'

The words made sense in Iris's head, and she realised herself that since Lorraine had been gone, Lachlan probably hadn't talked to anyone about this. All the fears and petty jealousy that had flitted through her mind vanished. She put her other hand over the one Lachlan had intertwined with hers. 'It sounds as if you were a very good friend to Lorraine. She must have appreciated everything that you did for her. It must have given her relief, knowing that she was living with someone who would do anything for her and follow her wishes.'

He nodded and let out a long, slow breath. 'I would have done anything for her. I just wanted her to be comfortable. When she finally died, I followed her wishes for her memorial and then…there was just nothing left for me.'

He looked almost embarrassed. 'I hated the house that we'd bought. I hated the view from the windows. I felt trapped there. All of my patients had known Lorraine. But they talked about her as if she'd been the great love of my life. To say anything else would have felt like a betrayal. We'd never really explained our relationship to anyone. It wasn't anyone else's business. I started to resent my job, and my patients, and knew I just had to get out of there.'

He turned to face her. 'So, coming here, to this place—finding that cottage, and getting this job—just seemed like all my dreams coming true.' He ran a hand through his hair. 'And then, there was you.'

'Me?' Her voice was shaking.

'You,' he said, and the way he looked at her made her heart soar.

'I'm glad you came here,' she said softly.

He smiled at her as she reached up and touched his cheek. 'And now we've talked,' he said. 'And got things out into the open.' He paused for a second, before looking at her with hopeful eyes. 'Do you think we could see where things take us from here?'

Her chest tightened as she nodded. She wanted to take this chance with Lachlan again. She wanted the chance to be with the person who made her feel whole. But the fact she had kept something else from him was eating away at her. He'd just told her a big part of his history. He'd lost someone he'd cared deeply about. And she believed every word. Lorraine might not have been the big love of his life, but he'd clearly had a lot of affection for her and looked after her. It all seemed right to Iris—and so

like Lachlan. She no longer had that tiny pang
of hurt or jealousy. She was simply sorry that
Lachlan had lost someone. It sounded as if he'd
pretty much done it all on his own, and that
made her want to hug him even more.

'I've missed you more than I could ever tell
you. I have so many regrets,' she admitted.

'No.' He shook his head. 'Let's just take it
from here. This could be good for us.'

Her heart was flipping over and over. She
wanted to tell him about Holly but was conscious that at any moment another member of
staff could walk into the room. When she told
him about Holly, she wanted it to be just them,
uninterrupted, so they really had a chance to
talk things through.

'I have an idea,' he said suddenly. 'Let's go
for a walk after work.'

'You're on until eight,' she said, trying not to
look panicked as she thought frantically what
to do with Holly.

'Eight will be perfect. Come back and we
can leave from here. It will just be starting to
get dark. There's some place I want to go. And
something I want to do with you.'

He was looking at her with such warmth that
she couldn't possibly say no. 'Okay, I'll come
back. I'll be back here for eight.'

He dropped a kiss on her lips. 'Perfect. Now,

let's see some more patients before the rest of them come hunting for us.'

Lachlan felt lighter. He'd shared with Iris about Lorraine and what he'd gone through in the last few years. And she'd been fine about it. She seemed to understand that he'd held Lorraine in a lot of affection, rather than being heartachingly in love with her.

No one could ever hold his heart the way that Iris could.

After spending the night with her last week, processing things and having their heart-to-heart tonight, he was keen to move things along. He didn't want to pretend with Iris. He wanted to wear his heart on his sleeve. He knew there was still so much underneath they would have to talk about again, and still come to terms with. Children would likely never happen naturally for them, and Lachlan had long since accepted that children may never be part of his life. But he didn't want to be afraid to bring up the subject with Iris; he wanted the opportunity for them to reach some common ground. She would always be enough for him—it was time for him to reiterate that, and it seemed like now she might finally be ready to hear it and accept it as the truth. Eight years was a long time. If she'd had a change of heart and wanted to con-

sider other options for a family going forward
he'd be willing to talk about it. Whatever they
were going to do, he was sure he wanted to do
it together. And tonight, he wanted to make it
a sign of their fresh start.

Dead on eight o'clock he threw his scrubs
into the locker room laundry and pulled back
on his jeans and navy polo shirt. Iris was waiting outside.

He walked out into the pleasant evening and
didn't bother to check who might be behind
him as he held out his hand to her. He was glad
when she didn't hesitate and let him lead her
along one of the streets away from the hospital.
The dim evening light was pleasant, the street
lights just starting to turn on. 'Where are we
going?' she asked.

She'd let her hair down again and was wearing jeans, trainers, a navy-blue jacket, and he
could see a hint of bright pink jumper at her
neckline.

'I hope you're not hungry, because this is
strictly a no food date. This is something else.'

Her nose wrinkled. 'I grabbed some food
when I got home. You said a walk, so I dressed
appropriately.' She raised her eyebrows. 'But
you better not try and hike me into the mountains.'

He shook his head and stopped at a coffee

shop that was clearly open late. 'Let's grab something to drink in case we get a little cold.'

She waited while he bought them both coffees, but still took her free hand as they headed down the street. This was her city. He was sure she would guess where they were going soon. But it didn't stop the wave of excitement that fizzed in his stomach.

It was strange. He'd been married to this woman for three years. He'd proposed to her in bed of all places. But tonight, he was even more nervous than he'd been all those years ago.

They started down towards the River Liffey and he suspected she thought he might be taking her over towards the main streets lined with bars. But as they walked along the side of the river, he realised he couldn't have hit a more perfect time.

The evening sky was dimming all the time and lights on the white bridge in front of them were glowing. There was green underneath at either side, with yellow and white towards the middle and reflecting off the dark river.

He stopped walking and turned to face her. She tilted her head to one side and looked at him quizzically. 'What?'

He nodded his head slowly. 'Okay, to some people this is just the pedestrian bridge from one part of Dublin to another. To others, this is the Ha'penny Bridge.'

She laughed. 'I've been over this bridge hundreds of times. Why have you brought me here?' She lifted one hand. 'You do know we're not allowed to put any of those lock things on it, don't you?'

He nodded. 'I know. I was thinking about something else. Something for us.'

He took her hand again and led her to the bridge. It was well used, and several other people were crossing at the same time. They walked into the middle of the bridge and he stopped, turning to face her again. He was certain the time to do this was now. It had come to him out of nowhere after what had happened today, and he'd wanted to mark something between them. He wanted to let her know how serious he was, and that he wanted an entirely clean slate for them to work from. Iris was the most important person in the world to him.

She swallowed nervously, wondering what Lachlan was about to do. She'd made an excuse to her neighbour that she had to run back to work and would likely be a couple of hours. But at some point, she needed to get back home to Holly.

He held up one hand to the scene around

them. 'So, we're in Dublin. I know you've lived here for a while, but for us, we have no history here.'

Iris gave a slow, thoughtful nod. That made sense. 'Okay.'

With her nod, enthusiasm seemed to grip him. 'So, we're over the River Liffey. It's a beautiful evening. We couldn't find a more perfect spot.'

Her heart skipped a few beats and she looked around. Surely he wasn't going to suggest something unexpected? They'd only just agreed to give things a chance. For a second, her mouth went dry. She still had to sit him down and spill out her whole heart to him—to tell him all about Holly and how her life had changed becoming a mother at last. It only took her a moment to realise they were entirely alone. The rest of the pedestrians had disappeared into the night. The sky was filled with deep mauves and the river seemed to twinkle with the reflected green, yellow and white lights. A few coloured buildings lined the side of the river. If she didn't know she was in Ireland right now, she might think she was on a movie set, or at a popular American theme park.

Lachlan pulled something from his pocket and this time her heart almost stopped. But it only took a second to realise what it was. An old-fashioned halfpenny. 'Where did you get that?'

Iris leaned forward. These hadn't been in circulation in her lifetime. She'd only ever seen them online before.

'I've had it for a while. My old auntie gave it to me as a good luck charm years ago. I found it when I was at the cottage the other night and thought it might mean something.'

'What do you mean?'

He pulled a sorry kind of face. 'My original thought was that we could come here and make a wish together and throw it into the river. Something to signify a new start for us.'

She smiled at him; honestly, this guy could touch her in places she didn't even know existed. Her fingers reached out to touch the shiny coin. She already knew there was a but coming.

'But?'

'But I thought that a ha'penny might not be too good for the river. So, I thought of something else instead.' He dug into his pocket and pulled out a small but perfectly formed flower.

Iris let out a gasp. 'Where on earth did you get that?'

He tapped the side of his nose. 'Never you mind. Just know, it was last minute, and I had to have some help.'

She leaned forward and looked closer. He

had a small perfectly formed peach-coloured rose. It looked as if it might have come from some kind of bouquet. 'What are we going to do with this?'

Lachlan pulled one small petal from the rose. He held it in his hand, then let it go over the water, mouthing a few silent words. He turned back and smiled. 'There,' he said in a deep voice, 'I've gone first. A wish and a promise for what might happen next.'

'But you didn't say it out loud.' She felt a bit cheated. 'I want to hear what you're wishing for.'

He gave her a smile. 'Okay.' He pulled another petal. 'This one is for a new promise between us. A chance to start anew.'

Hope filled her heart as he sent the little petal down onto the river. She leaned over and saw it carried on the current away from them.

She leaned over and plucked a petal herself. 'For a new beginning.' She copied his actions and let it fall from her hand.

'For no regrets,' said Lachlan, and did it again.

Her heart panged as she copied him. She meant it, she wanted to have no regrets between them.

'For love,' he said as he pulled her closer. 'I love you, Iris. I always have.' The heat from his body flowed to hers. She wrapped her arms around his neck and pressed her lips to his. She was secretly stunned. She hadn't been prepared for this. But as much as she loved this moment, it was never clearer to her that now was the time to tell him her whole truth. He knew part of her story about her upbringing and how it had impacted on her initial thoughts about adoption. Her fears, and the fact she had worked through them. But now he needed to know about Holly.

She let her lips move away from his and pulled another petal from the rose. 'For love,' she said as she held it in her fingers. 'Now and always.'

He grinned at her, picking her up and spinning her around. When he set her feet back on the ground, she wound her fingers through his hair. 'I can't remember the last time I was this happy,' he whispered in her ear.

'Me either,' she agreed. She took a deep breath and put her hands on his chest. 'But there's something else I want to talk about. Something that's really important. And I hope you'll understand.' Her stomach was currently doing backflips.

It must have been the expression on her face, either that or he could sense how nervous she was. He pulled back. 'You can tell me anything, Iris. No secrets between us.'

'No secrets.' She nodded in agreement and took a deep breath.

'Help!'

The scream made them jump apart instantly. Both of them turned. There was a man lying crumpled on the path by the river. Another man was by his side, grabbing at his friend and clearly trying to revive them.

Lachlan started running, and it took Iris a second to join him. She'd just been about to tell him—tell him about the most important aspect of her life. And now this. She pulled her phone from her pocket and dialled the number she needed. Lachlan was already on his knees performing CPR. The man who'd collapsed looked in his fifties and had the classic pallor of someone who'd had a myocardial infarction. She spoke to the emergency services, giving the situation and their exact location before kneeling down to assist.

For two emergency doctors the process of resuscitation was second nature. But frustration simmered just beneath the surface for both. They had no equipment, no drugs and no means to shock his heart back into rhythm. The odds of survival for cardiac arrest in the street were slim, but Iris was determined that this man would at least stand a chance.

The ambulance appeared quickly, with the two personnel jumping out. There was a nod of acknowledgement when it was clear they recognised both Iris and Lachlan. The man's condition didn't immediately improve, and when it was clear he would need to continue to be resuscitated, Lachlan looked at her with sorry eyes. She knew exactly what he wanted to do.

'Go.' She nodded. 'You need to help.'

'But what about you?'

She shook her head. This ambulance would be heading to another hospital that was slightly closer, not their own. And she knew she had to get home soon to Holly. She couldn't allow herself to get caught up in something else. Lachlan and the paramedic were more than capable of getting this guy to hospital.

'I'll see you later.' She was full of frustration and regret. But it wasn't the time and it wasn't the place. It just seemed like the last few chances when she'd wanted to tell him about Holly, something else always got in the way.

Lachlan climbed into the back of the ambulance with the man's friend, giving a swift wave of his hand. 'Talk later,' he said as the door closed.

She watched as the ambulance took off with

the lights flashing and gave a deep sigh. She'd promised Lachlan a fresh start. And she wanted that for them both. But the truth was, until she sat him down—without other distractions—and told him about her daughter, neither of them could ever have a fresh start.

And that made her heart hurt in a way it hadn't for years.

CHAPTER EIGHT

LACHLAN FINISHED THE EMAIL, asking the estate agent to put his house on the market back in England once the lease was up. There was no point keeping it. He would never go back there. Not now. He hadn't even managed to have that conversation with Iris yet. But he was sure she would be happy to hear he was staying in Dublin.

His hand brushed the inside rough brick of the cottage. He loved this place. Scout was currently rooting around his legs, apparently impatient to get back outside. Starting a new life with Iris again would undoubtedly mean leaving the cottage. Although he hadn't seen it, she clearly loved the red brick terraced house she'd bought in Portobello. Maybe he could persuade her to look at dog adoption? He'd quickly grown used to having Scout around and he enjoyed the fact of having a constant companion. He smiled as he took Scout for a final walk before heading to work. Ireland was bringing him a whole new life again. Part of him wondered what might have happened if he'd waited a few more weeks before making the decision back home that he'd had enough. This job would likely have been taken. He would have ended up somewhere else and never met Iris again. That made his stomach twist in a way he didn't like. Did he really believe in fate, or was this all just dumb luck?

An hour later he returned Scout to Maeve, giving her a quick, unobtrusive check over. Her meds had been changed after they'd discovered she had adrenal insufficiency. She had no other big symptoms of Addison's disease, but Lachlan, and her consultant at St Mary's, were keeping a careful eye on her.

'How's things with the beautiful Iris?' she asked. He'd quickly learned that Maeve would always be known for her persistence. She didn't let things go.

He gave a warm smile. 'Good. Better than good. Let's just see how things go.'

He moved over to her table where he glanced some paperwork. 'What's this?'

His eyes scanned the drawings.

But Maeve was still lost in romantic thoughts. 'Love reunited. I like that, it's like some old-fashioned love story.

'I'm thirty-four,' he laughed. 'I'm not completely out of the game yet.'

Maeve looked up. 'Oh, those.' She waved a hand. 'Before you moved in, I had big ideas. I fancied myself doing all those renovations that other people have done and leasing the place for a fortune.'

He blinked at the wall on one side of the large, extended cottage plans, made mainly of glass. A bit like the house up on the hill where the kids had got sick from the hot tub. It made him shiver.

'Maeve, far be it from me to comment, but the best part of the cottage is the natural features. The old-fashioned brick. The rough stonework.'

'What about the gaps around the windows and the irregular plumbing? I know you're there on your own, but what if you had more guests? There isn't much room.'

He nodded, his thoughts going to earlier. He didn't imagine he could persuade Iris to move to the cottage, but even if he did, it would be a tight fit for two. There was very little storage space, and he could almost hear her voice echoing in his ears: 'Where would I put the vacuum cleaner, or the ironing board?' Both things that he'd never had a requirement for in the last few weeks.

'You're right. There isn't much room. But is there any way you can extend but keep everything in the style it is now, with just a few subtle updates—' he smiled '—like the windows and the plumbing?'

She gave a nod. 'I suppose I could. But don't all the youngsters and trendy people want glass everywhere?'

Lachlan shook his head. 'I guess everyone is different. But I guess if I was picking a place to stay for a holiday, I would think your cottage was perfect. If I wanted to come with friends, I'd just want some more space. A few more bedrooms, a bigger sitting room and maybe another bathroom, and maybe another entrance where all the muddy boots could go after walking in the hills. Hey, can you hire Scout with the place?' he joked, bending down and scratching Scout behind the ears.

Maeve looked thoughtful for a few minutes. 'I might talk to the architect again. I'll see what he can come up with.' She looked back at Lachlan and grinned again. 'I made you a cake.'

'What?'

'For you, and your colleagues. Take it to work with you. It's on the counter in the kitchen in a metal tub for you. Irish apple cake.'

Lachlan's stomach immediately growled at the thought of it. 'You're supposed to be taking things easy right now. But I'll just say thank you and take it anyway. I'm hungry already.'

He smiled as he left and drove to the hospital. He deposited the cake in the staff lounge with a note on it and quickly changed and headed to the nurses' station. He'd been trying to think of some place local that he and Iris could go to in the next few days. There was still so much of Dublin he hadn't seen yet, and having his own personal guide would be a perfect bonus.

Iris was on duty, and he could hear her talking behind the curtains as she reviewed a patient. He grabbed the details of the next patient on the list—a woman with acute abdominal pain—and went to see her.

By the time he'd finished, Iris appeared looking a little flustered. 'Okay?' he asked.

She pressed her lips together. 'Can we get a chance to sit down together, maybe later on?'

'Do you want grab lunch together?'

She shook her head. 'No, not here. It's not something I want to talk about at work.'

Lachlan stopped for a second. 'Something wrong?'

The way she hesitated before answering was like a punch to the guts. 'Yes, no, maybe.' Iris looked distinctly nervous. It wasn't something he was used to seeing on her.

He reached out and took her hand, not caring who around here saw him. 'What's wrong?'

She sucked in her cheeks, then forced a smile on her face. 'Nothing. Let's just leave things until later. It's just really, really important that we have a chance to sit down together and talk, Lachlan. I've tried to talk to you a few times but something else always comes up.'

His guts churned. This wasn't like her. At least, not in any way he could remember. Perhaps she was going to tell him she didn't want to try again. He'd just reached the desk when the red phone began to ring. Lachlan had enough experience in A&E to know exactly what that meant. Someone was calling a major incident alert. It was midday, and it was during the week. This was unusual. Most major incidents happened at weekends or in the evening. All around him, other phones started to ring.

He kept calm. 'St Mary's.'

'Major incident alert. There's been a mudslide causing a train derailment. Ambulances just on-site. Casualty numbers will be available soon. St Mary's is listed as twenty major casualties. Can you confirm those numbers for me?'

Officially, Lachlan should check at this point with the head of the department in case there was anything else going on in the hospital that meant they wouldn't have room for the potential patients. But he didn't need to. He knew A&E was relatively quiet this morning. They could clear the patients they had in the next twenty minutes. 'Confirming St Mary's for twenty casualties.'

People had already gathered around him. He replaced the receiver and raised his voice. 'Train derailment. More details to follow. Confirmation of potential casualty numbers for St Mary's. We'll get a call back to let us know how many will actually be coming. Ambulances are on-site. So, it'll likely be soon. Can we clear our patients, and alert all other services? Speak to the surgeons, tell them they need to delay routine surgeries. We should know soon.'

Noise erupted around him. Joan appeared at his side with a checklist. She shouted orders to people like a military sergeant. He smiled and put a hand on her shoulder. 'Thank you.'

He saw a flash of yellow and Iris pushed her way through the people, her face pale. 'Was it a train? Was that what you said?'

He nodded. 'Mudslide, derailment.'

'What train? Where?'

He shook his head. 'They didn't say. But they'll get back to us shortly.'

Iris leaned against the wall and pulled her phone from her pocket. Her hands were shaking. Several people were asking him questions all at once, and Lachlan answered them as best as he could. 'Did they ask for an emergency team to attend the scene?'

He shook his head. It wasn't unusual in a major incident for ambulance services to ask for additional support. A&E teams were trained to attend if required.

He pushed his way over to Iris, putting his hand around her shoulders and taking her away from everyone else. The nearest place was the laundry store and he closed the door behind them. 'What's wrong?'

It wasn't just her hand that was shaking, it was her whole body. She tried to push past him. 'I need to find out. I need to find out about the train.'

He shook his head. 'Did you have a friend travelling by train today? Is that's what wrong?'

Her hand was still clutching her phone. The screen was lit and he could see she was on one of the well-known social media sites that gave a constant stream of news.

The words didn't seem to form on her lips. From the cupboard, Lachlan could hear the shrill ring of the red phone again. 'Let me get that,' he said, regretful that he'd have to leave her alone.

He strode quickly back to the desk and picked

up the phone just as Joan was about to. 'St Mary's.'

'We have seven casualties coming your way. Two major—both adults, one head injury, one multiple fractures. The five other casualties are schoolchildren aged between seven and ten. It seems there were three different primaries on a co-ordinated school trip.'

His hand gripped the receiver even tighter. His skin prickled. There was always something horrible about knowing children were involved in a major incident. 'Can you give me details of what train this was, in case we have enquiries?'

He listened carefully. When he'd finished, he replaced the receiver and repeated the news to the staff. 'Prepare for two adult majors, one with head trauma, one with multiple fractures. Five children all minor. See if we can get a pae-diatric team down here.'

Joan tugged his elbow. 'Five children?' She was frowning.

'Apparently some school trip.'

'What school?'

He shook his head. 'They didn't say. But there were three different primary schools on that train.'

'What train?'

He repeated what he'd been told and heard a strangled sound somewhere. Of course. He wasn't sure what school it was, or where it was situated in the city, but some of the staff in the hospital might have family members affected.

He moved his way through the people, watching faces, catching the flash of yellow in the distance heading into the treatment room. It was his favourite of her shirts. She looked good in it. Now it was calling him like a beacon.

All the staff around were moving dutifully to their places, preparing for their patients. Seven was actually quite a small amount following a major incident, and with only two with serious injuries, the department would be able to cope without problems. But what on earth was going on with Iris?

It might have been a few years, but he'd worked with her before when there had been major incidents. She was always calm and organised. He didn't recognise her right now.

He got stopped numerous times on the way to the treatment room, answering queries easily. Unusually, the door was closed. As she pushed it open he watched. Iris was leaning across the sink retching. Her words were coming out in between. 'She is on that train. She is on that train.' Joan was holding her hair back for her and rubbing her back. 'It will be fine,' she was murmuring in a low voice. 'She's probably lost her phone in the panic. That's why she's not answering. I'll see if I can get patched through to the commander. Find out if anyone has her name.'

Joan's eyes lifted and she started when she saw Lachlan standing there. She leaned forward and whispered something to Iris, who snapped her head back up and stood back from the sink. He couldn't ever remember seeing her look so distraught.

'I'll give you a minute,' said Joan. 'See what I can find out.'

Lachlan didn't quite get what was going on. Clearly the news hadn't gone down well with Iris, but she hadn't mentioned friends or relatives with kids, or anyone who worked on the trains, so he couldn't quite understand what was going on. Iris had never been the kind of person to panic or overreact to these kinds of situations.

He let the door close behind him, stopping himself from immediately holding her close. Something was telling him to wait. She looked terrible. He could see a snapped ponytail band on the floor and her blonde hair was in complete disarray all around her face.

He watched Iris carefully. Her breathing was ragged beneath her yellow shirt. 'Tell me,' he said. 'Tell me who you are worried about on that train. Who is on that train that has you in this state?'

He couldn't stop himself. He moved the few steps and put his arm around her. Iris's wide blue eyes looked at him. She looked as if her heart was in pieces. 'Holly,' she breathed. 'She's on that train. She's on a school trip. She's not answering her phone.'

Something lanced through his heart. He knew the answer before he asked the question. 'Who is Holly?'

There was only the briefest pause before Iris answered in a sob. 'My daughter.'

His brain went everywhere. The kids on the train were between seven and ten. He and Iris had split eight years ago. But no. Iris wasn't pregnant then. That was the reason they'd split up. So, if she'd had a child since then, she'd moved on from him pretty quickly.

Last night, they'd agreed to move forward and yet Iris hadn't told him she had a daughter. It was a pretty big non-disclosure. But he could get over it. He could. Even though he couldn't for the life of him understand why she wouldn't have mentioned her daughter before now. A child wasn't something to hide.

There wasn't time for this now.

'Okay,' he said calmly. 'Holly. Is her second name the same as yours—Conway? Can we ask ambulance control if they have her? Let's do that.' He was trying to be logical. Putting things in order in the way that Iris clearly couldn't right now. But she was a parent. She wasn't a doctor right now. And she was doing what any parent would—panicking while they waited to know if their child was okay.

He pushed everything else aside. This was too important.

'I meant to tell you. I was going to tell you. I was going to tell you tonight,' Iris sobbed, her whole body heaving. 'That's why I haven't invited you back to my place. I had to tell you about Holly.'

There was a definite wave of panic flooding through Lachlan. It was filling in any possible reason for Iris not telling him she had a daughter.

The age pinged again in his brain. Was Holly his daughter? Again, the possibility of Iris being pregnant with his baby when she left filled his irrational thoughts. The IVF had been over. But they'd still been sleeping together. Almost right up until the end. They'd never managed to get pregnant when they'd tried before, but could some quirk of fate have allowed her to become pregnant just before she left and they now had a seven-year-old daughter?

His head just couldn't compute that. Iris

would never have had their child and not told him. That was an unimaginable betrayal.

He couldn't ask the question. He couldn't ask it out loud. He touched her shoulder. 'You stay here. Let me find out what I can.'

He walked back out into the claustrophobic atmosphere of the department, his gut clenched solid. He moved over to Joan. 'Any news?'

She knew exactly what he was talking about, and didn't make any pretence about it. Something struck him. All these people must have known Iris had a child and none of them had mentioned it. Why not? Had she asked them to keep it a secret? He tried to dampen his anger down. He was starting to feel numb with shock.

Joan passed him a number. 'There's ambulances at the scene from all across Dublin and the surrounding areas. I'm on the phone to one depot. You try this one.'

He picked up the phone automatically and dialled. 'Hi, it's Lachlan Brodie, consultant at St Mary's. I'm trying to trace a child. Do you have a note of who is in all of your rigs following the train derailment? Yes, I'll wait.'

Joan glanced at him. 'You on hold?' He nodded. 'Me too. I hate this.'

He was finding it hard to look this woman in the eye. She was talking so easily to him.

How could she, if she'd deliberately been hiding a child from him?

It gave him a bit of reassurance. His mind was just racing away and making up stories. There was only one person that could tell him the truth, and she wouldn't be in any fit state to do that until she knew her daughter was safe.

Another phone rang; a nurse answered and gave a quick shout to her colleagues. 'Our two major trauma cases are arriving.'

Lachlan was torn. He'd told Iris to stay where she was, and she wasn't in a fit state to see patients right now. He put a hand on Joan's shoulder and handed her his receiver too. 'You do the phones, then check on Iris. I'll triage these first two patients and take care of them.'

Joan gave a nod of her head, and as he walked to the resus room he saw Rena already running through some drip lines.

Fergus came into the other side of the room and both he and Rena exchanged glances. They were expecting another doctor in here. They were expecting the head of their department. 'I'll run both cases,' said Lachlan without hesitation. 'I suspect both will end up in radiology since one has multiple fractures and one has a head injury. But full assessment first.'

It was only a few moments before both patients were rolled in. As he worked steadily alongside Rena and Fergus, he was confident that everything was being done for both patients. The older lady had been going on a day trip. She was conscious, with low blood pressure, probably due to her injuries. She'd broken her shoulder, her right arm and her right leg with the way the carriage had rolled. He suspected there might also be a few ribs involved. Thankfully, two of the orthopaedic surgeons were on hand quickly, to join in the assessment process and take her off to surgery. The second patient was a middle-aged man; he was dressed in a suit and had a large gash to his head and had been unconscious since he was found. His investigations showed a subdural haematoma, and a specialist surgeon was available to take him to Theatre to release the pressure on his skull.

As Lachlan was treating these patients, he was pleased to see a number of his colleagues from Paediatrics file past the door. Two doctors and an equal number of nurses from the ward had come down to help with the school-children. He wanted to go out and ask if Holly was among them, but he knew his priority had to be to treat these patients, so Iris was free to try and find her daughter.

Joan appeared at the door. 'We've several

more patients coming in. No majors. Equal numbers of adults and kids.'

'How many?' He was staring at her intently and she gave the tiniest shake of her head as she replied, 'Three of each. We'll cope. We have plenty of staff.' The message was there. Iris still didn't have news of Holly.

Lachlan waited until the man was wheeled out of Resus and snapped off his gloves. He took a brisk walk around the department, checking on every patient and all the staff working on them, making sure there were no problems and he was not needed.

Bays had been cleared for the new patients expected, and staff were ready. He moved into one of the bays where a young girl in a school uniform was getting her elbow stitched. 'You're every brave,' he said, giving a nod to the paediatrician stitching her. 'What's your name?'

'Ruby,' she answered. 'Is my mammy coming soon?'

The doctor stitching looked up and smiled. 'She'll be here soon. I've spoken to her. I told you that.'

He really wanted to ask Ruby if she knew Holly, but he also knew just how inappropriate that was. He glanced at Ruby's school jumper sitting on the nearby chair. The school name and badge were easy to see: St Regent's.

'Are my friends okay?' asked Ruby. He wanted to send a silent signal of thanks upwards. It was just the opening he needed.

'Give me the names of some of your friends and I'll see if I can find out how they are.'

Ruby rattled off a whole host of names. Even if he'd had a notebook and pen in his hand he couldn't have kept up. But one of those many names was Holly.

He held up his hand. 'Holly Conway?'

Ruby nodded.

'Were you all sitting together?'

Ruby shook her head. 'Mrs McLellan made us go in pairs. She did it by names. We didn't get to sit together. I wasn't next to any of my friends.' There was a distinct amount of pouting.

'Okay.' Lachlan nodded. 'I'll try and find out which of your friends are here.'

He gave a nod to the other doc and went back to the treatment room, but it was empty and the door was lying wide. He scanned the department and couldn't see any sign of the yellow shirt. Where was she?

It only took a few more tries to find her. She was in one of the rarely used offices, on the phone to one of the other emergency departments.

He could see the list in front of her with the

names scored off in turn. As she replaced the receiver her shoulders sagged. 'I can't find her. No one knows where she is. She isn't in any of the other hospitals, and no ambulance has her.' It was clear the frustration was driving her crazy.

'Will they let us go to the site?'

She shook her head. 'I've tried that. The police say no way. They're still pulling people out. What if she's trapped there, scared and alone? Why can't I get to my baby?'

It didn't matter how many questions of his own Lachlan had right now. He wrapped his arms around her and let her sob on his shoulder.

He couldn't think what else to offer to do. Part of him burned. If this was his child, what would he do? The thoughts played on his mind. He took a deep breath. 'Let me call ambulance control again. Maybe we're asking the wrong questions.'

He still remembered the number from earlier and dialled again. 'Lachlan Brodie from St Mary's. The children on the train who weren't injured. Where have they been taken? And what arrangements have been put in place to contact the families?' He listened carefully. 'So, they've all been checked over by your staff. Do you want to bring them all to St Mary's for a second opinion, or at least a central waiting place? We have room here.' He actually didn't know that. And he didn't care. He didn't baulk when the commander at the ambulance station told him he didn't need a second opinion. However, the offer to take the children away and co-ordinate the return to their parents was a different story. It wasn't just St Regent's children that had been on the train. There had been two other schools, all on a co-ordinated trip. Even though the police were helping too, they had children in a variety of places. Getting them all in one place would help. Apparently, that would free up some of their staff that were needed for other duties. Lachlan replaced the receiver. He stuck his head out of the door. 'Anyone seen Rose?'

Two minutes later, Rose Reid, the hospital general manager, appeared. He held out his hand and took hers, shaking it, and not letting go. 'Don't kill me.'

Her brow narrowed. 'What have you done?'

'I've offered to take the uninjured children off ambulance control so they can keep dealing with casualties. Apparently, there are a number of kids that they need to contact the parents for. I told them we had space and staff to assist.'

Rose raised her eyebrows. He'd seen her dashing about for the last few hours, helping wherever she could. He hoped he hadn't played this wrong. She waved a hand. 'Is that all? No problem at all. I'll take them all along to the paediatric outpatient clinic. Plenty of things to keep them amused. I'll get some food from the kitchen and some admin staff to get in touch with the schools to see how best to assist.' He saw her gaze go to Iris behind him. She lowered her voice. 'Anything else I can do to help?'

He shook his head. 'The controller said the children will come with a police escort.'

Rose nodded. 'Give me five minutes and I'll be ready. I'll send some staff round to help take the children along to outpatients.'

Rose disappeared out the door and Lachlan turned to look at Iris again. Last night, they'd stood on a bridge and tossed rose petals onto the river, along with all their promises and wishes for the future. How could he create a future with someone who kept secrets from him—possibly the biggest secret of all?

Right now, he walked over and put his hand on Iris's shoulder. 'Why don't we go and wait for those schoolkids to arrive?'

Iris swallowed nervously. It was clear she was still trying her best to keep calm. She nodded and followed Lachlan to the entrance to the department. There was so much he wanted to ask her. So much he wanted to say. But he still understood that now wasn't the time. For all he knew, Holly might not be among these children. She could—as Iris dreaded—still be trapped on the train.

A police car pulled up, with a few police vans behind. Lachlan moved over to greet the lead officer, just as an admin staff member hurried to join him. They exchanged a few words and he was conscious of Iris, her eyes fixated on the faces in the vans. The doors opened and the children started to climb out. A few were nonchalant, others looked bedraggled, a few others slightly stunned; all were dressed in some form of uniform, with or without jackets, and one young boy had only one shoe.

Lachlan moved over next to them, ushering them all to follow him. At just the right moment, Rose Reid appeared and clapped her hands, telling them all she'd look after them until their parents could come for them. One of the Guardai moved over to join her and between them they started to filter the children along. The admin staff took names as the children got to the entrance. But Lachlan knew that Iris wasn't waiting for a name. She'd started to pace, staring into the various vans, frantically searching for her daughter. After a few seconds she let out a yelp and hugged a little girl who stepped down from a van. His heart leapt in his chest until he heard the words. 'Esther, I'm so glad to see you.' She clasped both of the little girl's cheeks before giving her another giant hug. 'Let me look at you again, are you okay?' The little girl nodded.

'Is Holly with you?'

Esther shook her head. 'She's in another van. Can you call my mammy?'

The spark of light that flared in Iris's eyes was obvious from even a few steps away. He could see her breathe a huge sigh of relief. Someone had seen her daughter alive and well. This little girl had told her she was in another van, which likely meant she was uninjured, and on her way. He watched Iris blink back tears as she pulled her phone from her pocket and started talking rapidly to someone. 'Frank. Esther's here. She's fine. She's just been brought to St Mary's to co-ordinate collection for the parents.' She let out a nervous laugh. 'No, I've not seen Holly yet, but Esther tells me she's in another van.' Iris handed the little girl over to the member of admin staff. 'Esther Reilly, St Regent's Primary. Don't worry, I'm talking to her *daidi* now.'

She reluctantly let Esther go, then spun back around to watch the other vans appear. It was a slow process. Since the vans were coming from a few different venues, they all arrived at different times.

Lachlan was nervous. He couldn't pretend that he wasn't.

As one van after another pulled up, he helped the children down, casting a careful eye over them, and giving a nod to the staff for the ones that seemed upset. At last a van pulled in and he sensed Iris's emotions straight away. 'Holly,' she breathed, clearly spotting her daughter's face at one of the windows.

She started waving frantically as large tears poured down her cheeks.

He wasn't quite sure what to do with himself, or what to think about the way his heart currently felt like a clenched fist.

The admin assistant was being methodical with the kids. Every time a child set foot from a bus, she took a name, a school and a date of birth if they knew it. He wondered if she would bypass all this when Holly was obviously Iris's.

Iris couldn't wait; as soon as the doors opened on the bus she ran straight up the steps and disappeared from view. Lachlan pretended his throat wasn't bone dry, and his heart rate wasn't pounding in his ears.

She had a right to reunite with her child in private.

He kept telling himself that, as the minutes seemed to stretch on for ever. A few other kids came off the bus, and he moved beside the admin assistant, casting a quick eye over them all.

Finally, a tear-streaked Iris appeared, her eyes bright with relief, with a little girl tucked under her arm.

Lachlan breathed deeply, not sure what he could say. But Iris stepped down and rattled off details to the admin assistant: Holly's name, school and date of birth.

The date of birth registered in his brain instantly. Holly was seven, so the dates didn't quite fit. He couldn't rationalise the wave of emotions that rolled over him. There was no way she was his daughter, and he didn't know if he was sad, or relieved.

His heart sunk like a stone, and his brain couldn't compute. If Holly had been his daughter and Iris had hidden her for years, then he would have been unimaginably angry. Now he knew that wasn't a possibility, so why did he still feel a knot of cold fury deep inside him?

This whole thing was making him crazy.

'Do you want me to check her over?' he asked Iris through tight lips.

For a moment, she paused. He could see a million emotions flitting across her eyes. But being a parent came above everything else. 'Yes,' she breathed.

* * *

He knelt down. 'Hi, Holly, I'm Lachlan, one of the doctors that works with your mum. Bring her with you and we'll make a quick check to make sure you're okay.'

Holly pulled her head out from where it was carefully tucked into Iris's side. She was a frail, pretty little thing with light brown long hair, brown eyes and freckles on her face.

He gave her a reassuring smile and Holly gave him an unsure glance.

He held out his hand to let them go inside in front of him. There was a squeal and he watched as Joan appeared out of nowhere and wrapped Holly in a hug. She started talking rapidly to Iris, and dropped a kiss on the top of Holly's head, before glancing back at Lachlan. Her eyes flitted between Iris and Lachlan as if she didn't really understand what was going on.

'I'm going to give Holly a quick check. Why don't you help me?' He could see Joan's professional status slide back into place.

'Of course,' she agreed, then picked the seven-year-old up in her strong arms and carried her over to the nearest cubicle, perching her on the edge of one of the examination trolleys.

Lachlan let his years of experience take over. This wasn't a time for unwelcome emotions.

Iris was a colleague, whose child had been involved in a major incident. Although he was sure the ambulance personnel had checked all these kids properly—for a colleague, he would always check again.

Joan spoke quietly in his ear. 'One of the paediatric doctors is around at outpatients, just keeping an eye on all the children before their parents come.'

He nodded. She'd read his mind. Someone from this hospital was checking all these kids. Kids were a resilient bunch. But sometimes symptoms, particularly emotional and psychological impacts, weren't immediate. Right now, he had no idea what any of these children had seen or been exposed to. They knew there were some serious injuries, but he still didn't know if there had been any fatalities at the scene.

He took out his pen torch and showed it to Holly. 'Do you know what this is?'

Joan was helping her out of her school cardigan. 'My mum is a doctor,' Holly said in a quiet voice.

'Okay, then. You know what it is. I'm going to take a quick look in your eyes, if that's okay.'

Holly gave a nod as Joan slipped a pulse oximeter on to her finger.

Iris was standing silently, but he could see

her breathing easing. Her eyes never left her daughter for a second.

Lachlan kept things methodical, checking Holly for any unidentified injuries. Her observations were all entirely normal, and apart from a few marks on her arms and legs, where it was likely bruises were starting to form, there seemed to be nothing out of the ordinary.

When he'd finished, Joan gave Holly another hug. 'Do you want some chocolate?'

Holly glanced quickly at her mum, and then nodded. 'I lost my bag,' she said in a tiny shaky voice. 'It had my phone in it. And I don't know where my blazer is.'

It was almost like she'd just remembered these things. Delayed reactions could be common in children involved in accidents. Iris knelt down in front of Holly. 'Your bag, phone and blazer can be replaced. I'm just glad that you're safe, honey. I was *so* worried about you.'

Holly hugged her mother tight. Lachlan immediately felt like he was intruding on the family reunion. 'Everything looks good,' he said, picking up the chart with Holly's details. 'How about you two go home?'

Iris gave a grateful nod.

Lachlan wasn't sure how to feel about anything. The woman that he'd realised he loved on the bridge and had wanted to plan a future with only last night had lied to him. It might have been by omission. But it was still a lie.

As if she were reading his mind, Iris shot a glance in his direction. 'We'll talk tomorrow,' she said as she helped Holly back into her cardigan.

He watched as Iris walked out the department, hand in hand with her daughter, and he couldn't understand why his heart ached so badly.

She'd wanted this for so long. And he'd wanted it for her too.

So why did it hurt so much?

CHAPTER NINE

AT MIDNIGHT IRIS received a text.

I'm glad your daughter is safe. But we definitely need to talk. Tomorrow.

There was no question mark. It wasn't a question. It was a statement and she understood entirely why.

Iris couldn't sleep anyway. This had been the worst day of her life. The feeling of being powerless—to get information, or to help Holly in any way—had almost destroyed her.

Part of her felt a bit pathetic. But her stomach had ruled her at the beginning, and the tears of frustration had spilled over when it felt as if no one could really help her find her daughter. Rena had talked sharply to her when she'd wanted to jump in the car and drive on down to the scene of the accident, holding her by the shoulders, and telling her not to get in the way of the emergency services doing their jobs. What if her actions affected the welfare of someone else's child? It had been a blunt reminder of the types of conversations she'd had to have with patients' relatives over the years, and she'd hated every second of being at the receiving end for once.

She also hated that Lachlan had found out this way. She'd wanted the chance to sit down and tell him calmly about Holly. About how she'd come to be a mother, and how fabulous Holly was. They hadn't even formed the conversation about family again after their previous history.

It had probably seemed too soon to Lachlan to have those conversations. But Iris had known better. And she should have done something about it.

She'd seen the look of confusion in his eyes today. She'd seen the hurt. It was as clear as day. But he didn't even know the real story yet, and although she hated it, there was a good chance it might hurt him even more.

As she watched her daughter sleep, Iris was sure of one thing. She and Holly were a package deal. No matter how he felt at the news, Lachlan needed to understand that any relationship with Iris would be a relationship with

Holly too, and her stomach twisted at what the outcome of that conversation might be.

School was off tomorrow for obvious reasons. And she just wasn't prepared to leave Holly on her own. Her little girl hadn't spoken much about the accident since she'd got home. Just pushed her scrambled egg about her plate, eaten only a few mouthfuls, then asked if she could go to bed. She was clearly physically and emotionally drained. And Iris's priority was to be her mum. She couldn't invite Lachlan here. Not when she was unsure how he might react to the news she still had to tell him. So, whether he liked it or not, Lachlan Brodie was going to have to wait. In another day, she could meet him at one of the local cafés. Somewhere neutral they could talk, with no one else around. It might not be what he wanted. But it would have to do.

Lachlan hadn't really slept in the last two days. Yesterday, he'd done an extra shift at A&E to cover—and to keep his mind from other things. Even Scout couldn't cheer him up on the two long walks they'd taken across the country fields. His mind was working overtime and he fully acknowledged that wasn't doing him a bit of good.

As he approached the café in Portobello, he

could see Iris already sitting there. Her hair was around her shoulders and she was wearing a green jumper. He hated that his heart always skipped a few beats at every sight of her. What he really needed right now, and what he deserved, was answers.

She looked up anxiously as the door clang signalled his arrival. He slid into the seat opposite her at the window table in the café, far enough away from other tables that their conversation wouldn't be overheard.

When the waitress approached, he only ordered coffee, not even sure if his stomach would take that.

Iris was clearly nervous.

'How's Holly?'

'She's good, thanks. Her bruises have come out now, and she's a bit stiff and sore. Most of her friends who were in the accident are all okay. One was knocked out, but has recovered, one broke a wrist, another their tibia. The teacher's assistant seemed to get the worse of things. She was trapped for a while and had to be cut out. I'm not sure exactly what her injuries are.'

'Did Holly see anything she shouldn't have?'

Iris shook her head. 'I don't think so. Most of them were just in shock, really. They were disorientated after the carriage rolled and didn't know which way to get out. Thankfully there were a few businessmen on board, all standing near the doors. So, they stopped the kids getting off until they knew things were safe.'

The waitress appeared with the coffee and left it on the table, leaving them both in an awkward silence.

Iris looked up, her pale blue eyes on his. 'I guess I should tell you about Holly now.'

'I guess you should.' His words came out tight and he couldn't help it. He sat back in the chair. 'You should know that when I first heard about her, I wondered if she was mine.'

Iris's eyes widened in shock. 'What? Why would you ever think that? I would never have done that to you.'

He shrugged his shoulders. 'The kids were aged between seven and ten. We parted ways eight years ago. It did occur to me that you might have been pregnant when we split, and just not told me. It wasn't until I saw her date of birth and saw when she turned seven, that I realised we were out by several months.'

It was clear that the possibility of him thinking this had never even entered Iris's mind. She tried to reach out her hands towards him but flinched as he pulled them back.

'No, Lachlan. Absolutely not. I would never do that. Never.' Her expression was sincere, but even though the words should have helped, they didn't.

'But you didn't tell me about the daughter you did have. Even though we were dating again. Even though we'd slept together.'

He said it as a statement, although it was actually so laden with reined-in emotion that Iris winced. 'I know, I'm sorry. You're absolutely right. You have to know I had every intention of telling you. But I just couldn't find the right time.'

'Before we fell into bed might have worked. Or before we made those promises on the bridge. I didn't think I was making a whole host of promises to a woman who was keeping such a huge secret from me.'

Iris put her head in her hands. He knew he was being hard on her, but he was also being honest. Until they'd talked things through truthfully, he couldn't possibly know if there could be any hope for them going forward.

'I'm sorry,' she said, shaking her head. 'I intended to tell you after we slept together, but things got snarled up once I explained about my childhood to you, and then suddenly we had to get to work. Then, I was absolutely going to tell you on the bridge, but that man became unwell and I just didn't get the chance.'

He paused for a second, then spoke again. 'I

assume you met Holly's father not long after we split up?'

Her face was blank for a few moments, then she shook her head frantically. 'No, not at all.' He couldn't understand why her face looked even more pained. 'Holly isn't my biological child,' she said carefully.

Now Lachlan's brain jumped all over the place—all in a few seconds. He'd already had pictures in his head of Iris being pregnant. He had no reason to think anything else. He just assumed that the reason he and Iris couldn't get pregnant together was because they weren't a good biological match. It had always been in his head that there was a chance she could get pregnant with someone else, and he, in turn, could have had a family with someone else.

The idea that she hadn't been pregnant at all just didn't make sense. His brain searched for other family members. Iris didn't have brothers or sisters with children that she could have been left to care for. He couldn't even remember any cousins. Had a good friend maybe passed away? It was the only thing that made sense.

'What do you mean Holly isn't your biological child?' he asked.

She licked her lips nervously. The coffee in front of him had already gone cold and he hadn't even taken a sip. Iris rested her head on one hand. Now, she bit her bottom lip. He knew she was stalling.

'I mean… I adopted Holly.'

He froze. 'What?' It was the last thing he'd expected to hear. Every hair on his arms stood on end.

'I know you tried to talk to me about adoption. I know I was dead against it, for reasons I hope you understand now. But after we split, and I spent some time on my own, I started to re-evaluate things. It took a long time, with the help of a good counsellor, but after a number of years, I finally felt ready. I applied for adoption and spent over a year being assessed. Holly was placed with me when she was four. I adopted her three years ago.'

He could swear there was roaring in his ears right now. So many thoughts whirling for space in his brain. It was like he couldn't quite process what he'd heard. The words just seemed to have tumbled out of her in quick succession—as if she couldn't say them rapidly enough.

He leaned across the table towards her. 'But you were always so against it. The reason I didn't push for adoption was because I suspected you had issues you weren't ready to share. I let it go because you meant more to me. Even though it was a route I wanted to explore. When you said no, so completely, so absolutely, I knew I could live the rest of my life happily with just you.' He was shaking his head the whole time he was talking. It just seemed so incredible to him. 'So, I put the idea to bed. Because it was what you wanted. It was always about what you wanted, Iris. But it turns out you were keeping a whole host of secrets from me.' He sat back. All he could feel was disbelief and disappointment. 'If only you'd told me the truth. If only you'd confided in me—told me about your childhood experiences and your fears about adoption. We could have worked through them together, with a counsellor. We could have done all this together. Eight years. Eight years of our lives together lost, because you wouldn't talk to me, trust me.'

She looked stunned. But she couldn't be. What on earth had she expected him to say? This wasn't a punch to the guts—this was being dumped on by steel block. After refusing to listen to him, after not even considering the possibility of adoption, she'd gone off, and taken that option on her own. Without him. He was a fool. An absolute fool.

Tears sprung into her eyes, but he was done with Iris crying. She'd ripped his heart clean out of his chest. He hadn't thought that was even possible any more. Oh, how little he had learned.

'Please, Lachlan, let me explain. I just wasn't ready to accept that path when I was with you. I couldn't think straight, I couldn't sleep, I couldn't do anything because I was an emotional mess. The whole IVF thing just finished me off. Finding out we couldn't conceive without any real reason absolutely ruined me. I needed the science. I needed the facts. It would have been a million times better if it had been my fault, if I had blocked tubes, or no eggs. Or your fault, with sperm that couldn't swim. But telling us that everything was fine, just not when we were together, made me feel like such a failure. Useless. Worthless. I hated myself so much that I saw no other way out than for us to split up; I wanted you to be free to have what you always wanted—a child of your own. The one thing I couldn't give you. I couldn't even begin to think about adoption, especially after my upbringing. I wasn't ready. It took me three full years to sort myself out, Lachlan, before I started the process of becoming an adoptive parent. That's when I finally accepted myself for who I was and focused on making things work for me. We'd lost touch by then. I had no idea where you were in the world.'

He didn't speak. He didn't say a single word. Because he couldn't find any.

The woman he was looking at had been the

person he'd loved most in this world. The person he'd hoped to build a life with again, here, in Ireland. Coming here and finding her again had been like being gifted a whole new start. How much of a fool he had been.

Iris was panicking. Even though he was right across the table from her, she could see Lachlan retreating further and further away from her.

Nothing she said was right.

She was grasping at straws, struggling to put their history and the last eight years into some kind of perspective for him. But the explanation she was giving him seemed poor, even to her. What she wanted to do was to reach out and grab hold of Lachlan. Tell him that she loved him with her whole heart. That meeting him again had lit her up in a way she never thought possible.

The worst part was the hurt she could see all over his face. And she was the cause of that. She should have told him straight away about Holly.

'I'm sorry, Lachlan. I just wasn't ready to hear you back then. But you were right. You were absolutely right all along. I should have considered adoption. It was a real option for us, although I couldn't see that at the time. Believe me, I will always regret that. Just like I'll always regret not fighting harder for us. I just didn't have the energy or the belief in myself any more. My counsellor eventually made me see I'd been suffering badly from depression and not realised it at the time. I just thought the low mood, the lack of concentration and energy, the lack of appetite was all due to the effects of the IVF, and the subsequent failures. I thought being miserable was an entirely normal state of mind. I couldn't focus on anything else.'

Lachlan's face remained blank, almost frozen. It was like he'd stopped listening to her. And she should understand that, because eight years ago that had been her, shutting down and not listening to him.

But then he focused his gaze on her. 'I asked you speak to someone about it. I begged you to talk things through with a professional counsellor.'

She closed her eyes for a second. 'I know that. I know you did. But, Lachlan, what can I say? I wasn't myself. I didn't feel like myself. Now, I feel like I did when we were first together. Obviously I'm older, and hopefully wiser. And now I'm a mum.'

She pressed her lips together, realising how hard this had to be for him.

'You looked me in the eye the other night on

the bridge and made a whole host of promises to me, based on a life you hadn't told me about. It was all a lie, Iris. How can I ever trust someone who keeps secrets like that? Your daughter. She should never be a secret to keep—you should be shouting about her from the rooftops.'

He just looked entirely disgusted by her and it made her even more uncomfortable. She pressed her hand to her heart. 'Of course I should. And I do.'

'Did you ask all your colleagues to lie on your behalf?'

She cringed and sucked in a deep breath. 'Not exactly.'

'Not exactly?' Icy sarcasm dripped from his voice.

'I simply asked them not to discuss my personal life when you first arrived.'

'So, the first thing you thought about doing when we met again was lying to me about where you were in life. Nice.'

'Don't make it sound like that. I just thought this would be a difficult conversation. I remember how good you were about everything. I remember how you wanted to look at adoption, and I didn't know how to tell you that I'd gone ahead and done it myself.' She lowered her head. 'Because even to me, that seemed awkward and we had to work together for three months.'

Iris shook her head. She had to try and get back some control of this conversation. She had to make sure Lachlan knew exactly how she felt about everything.

'Adopting Holly has truly been the best thing I've ever done. I might have made a mess of this with you, but I won't make a mess of anything to do with Holly. We're a package deal. If you can find it in your heart to understand why I kept this from you, I'd need you to be happy to be a part of both of our lives, not just a part of mine.'

He blinked and looked at her.

'Holly isn't the problem.' His voice was deathly low and the look in his eyes froze her. 'You knew exactly how I'd feel about this. You didn't want to be together eight years ago. I've had to live with that. We couldn't have children together naturally. I lived with that too, and accepted it. You've had every right to live your life however you've wanted for the last eight years—just like I have too. But at least I was honest with you about what happened in my life. I told you about Lorraine, my career change and my reason for ending up back here. I felt as if I owed you that—' he put his hand on his heart '—because I wanted this to work.

I wanted to take this second chance for you and me and find a way to make it work.'

'And I do too.' She reached for him again, but Lachlan snatched his hands from the table, as if he couldn't bear her touch. 'I love you, Lachlan. I love you with my whole heart. Tell me how to make this work. Tell me how to make this right with you.'

'I can't get the past the fact you looked me in the eye, spent time with me, made promises to me, *made love with me*, and didn't tell me about one of the most essential parts of your life. That you adopted a child makes my head explode—probably because you shut down that option cold for us. But more than that, I can't think how on earth you thought I'd be so shallow as to only want my own biological children. Didn't you know me at all, Iris? Where on earth did those thoughts come from? The one thing you should always, always have known is that I am *not* like your parents.'

She looked a bit stunned, but he continued, fury driving him on. 'I absolutely know you have every right to make your own choices, time has moved on, and things changed for you. But in here?' He put his finger up to his head, then put his fist to his chest. 'And in here? I just see the woman I thought I loved again who couldn't be honest with me about the most important thing in her life. Who supposedly couldn't find one moment to tell me about her daughter's existence. Haven't you learned anything about keeping secrets? You've already torn my heart out once, Iris. I have no intention of hanging around for you to do it again.'

Before Iris could get a chance to say another word, Lachlan stood up and walked from the café.

She was shell-shocked. She knew she'd brought this all on herself. But somehow, she'd thought she might be able to make him understand. She'd no idea that he might have considered that Holly could be his daughter. It hadn't even occurred to her. Now she felt worse than ever. She should have spoken to Lachlan sooner about all this. But until that moment on the bridge, she hadn't really realised that he was going to tell her he loved her and wanted to start all over again.

Lachlan had truly pictured a life for him— for them—in Ireland, and she'd just snatched it all away from him.

Iris sagged her head down into her hands. She couldn't have made a bigger mess of this if she'd tried. How could she repair the damage that she'd done?

CHAPTER TEN

IRIS WAS GOING through the motions. Turning up at work, treating her patients and going home again. The atmosphere at work was terrible. Everyone knew that she and Lachlan weren't speaking. The staff were tiptoeing around them all. She'd heard Rose talking to someone else, saying that Lachlan had enquired about ending his contract early. Rose had told him if he left before they found a replacement it would put stress on the department. But knowing that he was trying to get away from a place he could easily have settled in—and it was all her fault—made her feel a thousand times worse. She'd tried to speak to him a few times, but Lachlan had made it clear their relationship was strictly professional.

Most of all, she missed him. Spending all her time with Holly would always be wonderful, but even Holly had noticed something was wrong.

'Why are you so sad, Mum?'

'I fell out with a friend even though I didn't mean to.'

'Can't you just say sorry?'

'I did, honey. But he's not happy with me. I'm not sure I can fix it.'

Holly forehead creased and she looked up from her schoolwork. 'Well, that's really sad. Maybe you just need to give him some time to think about it.'

Iris looked at her in surprise. 'Where did you hear that?'

'Mrs McLellan. When there are fights at school, she makes everyone say sorry. But we aren't always friends again until the next day. She says sometimes people need a little time to think things through.'

Iris smiled and rubbed her daughter's back. 'Well, I think Mrs McLellan is very wise. I guess I'll just need to wait and see how things go.'

Holly leaned her head on her hand. 'Which person at work is it? Is it Fergus? Or is it the new one?'

Iris smiled. There wasn't much she could get past her daughter. 'It's the new one, honey. His name is Lachlan.'

'The girls at my school said he was cute.'

'What?'

'He helped some of them at the hospital. Then he went along and talked to some of them when they were waiting for their mums and dads.'

'That's because he's a very nice man.' Iris smiled again sadly. 'And I wish I hadn't upset him. But you're right. I just need to give him some time.'

Holly wrinkled her nose. 'That bad smell is coming in our house again.'

'What bad smell?' Iris stood up and put her hands on her hips, sniffing deeply. Holly was right. There was a bad smell—one she didn't like.

'The one from earlier. We smelled it walking home from school today and out in the back garden. It's yucky.'

Iris's skin prickled—her senses suddenly alight. She turned to Holly. 'Honey, maybe we should...'

But she never got to finish the sentence before a huge boom echoed somewhere and she was blown from her feet.

Lachlan put the fifth apple cake that Maeve had baked for his colleagues into the staff lounge. It didn't matter how often he told her to rest, the woman seemed incapable of listening.

It didn't help matters that she was as astute

as they come. She'd been badgering away at him the last two weeks. Asking him what was wrong, if he wanted to talk about things, what had happened between him and Iris. The expression 'being like a dog with a bone' didn't come close. Maeve should have probably been a private investigator.

In the end, she stopped asking questions, and started nagging him. It was the only word he could use to describe it.

'You're clearly miserable. Whatever has happened between you and Iris, you need to get over it and make things right.'

When that didn't work, she tried a different approach.

'The first time around didn't work with Iris—are you going to let the second time slip through your fingers too?'

It was clear she was getting exasperated by his closed lips.

'You're torturing yourself seeing her every day. There needs to be an end to this—a line in the sand. Make up your mind, Lachlan, are you in, or are you out?'

This time he'd snapped.

'I'm out, and I wish you'd stop going on about it. Since when did you become Team Iris?'

A smile had hinted at Maeve's lips and he realised she'd got what she wanted—she'd tricked him into talking about it. She straightened in her chair. 'I'm not Team Iris. I am, and always will be, Team Lachlan. But it seems like my team doesn't know what's good for it. So, as an older friend, I feel obliged to point out the glaringly obvious—that you need to talk to her.'

His shoulders had sagged. 'I've done that. She disappointed me. She let me down. She wasn't honest with me when she should have been. Talking gets me nowhere.'

Maeve had nodded her head. 'You talked, but did you listen?'

He'd looked at her. 'What do you mean?'

Maeve had folded her hands in her lap. 'You know exactly what I mean. Now, pick up the cake from the kitchen.'

And just like that the conversation had been over and it had bothered him ever since.

Fergus appeared at his shoulder. 'More of Maeve's Irish apple cake?'

Lachlan nodded and pushed the tin in his direction. 'Help yourself. How are things out there?'

Fergus pulled a face. 'It's one of those days where you know not to say anything.'

Lachlan groaned. It was a well-known fact, in A&E departments across the world, that if you ever made the mistake of saying 'things were quiet,' it was like a licence for chaos.

He walked through to the front of the department, quickly checking the boards. He already knew Iris wasn't on duty today, and it was a relief to know there would be no awkward exchanges.

He was considering his position here. He had to. He'd thought Ireland was the perfect place for him, the perfect place for a new start. He loved his job again, liked the people he worked with, and finding Iris had made it feel as if all the jigsaw pieces that had been jumbled for the last eight years had finally settled into place.

Until the mudslide and train derailment and he'd found out she'd been keeping secrets.

Some of his self-reflection in the last few days had made him uncomfortable. He'd been thinking a lot about how Iris had spent the last three years bringing up Holly as a single mother, and the journey she'd taken to get to that stage. A tiny part of him wondered if he was actually a little bit jealous—and that didn't make him like himself much at all. He would have loved to have kids. Whilst others might run at the thought, he'd always wanted a family. His heart was big, he had a lot of love to give, and he couldn't help but envy the life that Iris had been able to give to Holly.

He heard running footsteps and turned around to see Fergus again with a phone in his hand. 'Anyone seeing these?' he shouted, his voice carrying across the department.

One of the admin staff stood up. She was talking on her mobile. She also reached for the remote for the TV that played in the patient waiting room.

The news wasn't playing, but a ticker tape message was running along the bottom of the screen.

Report of unidentified explosion in Dublin

There was a collective hush as people appeared from everywhere, pulling phones from pockets. The admin worker lowered her phone. 'My husband says it's in Portobello.'

Lachlan's skin went cold. They must have waited a few seconds before the department phones started to ring.

He snatched receiver up. 'St Mary's.'

'St Mary's, explosion of unknown origin confirmed in the Portobello area of Dublin. Residential area. No known casualty numbers as yet. Please confirm your ITU status.'

'Four beds available.' He signalled to a staff member to make the call to the ITU department.

'Two mobile teams required. Can you confirm?'

He knew every eye in the place was on him. 'Confirming two mobile teams from St Mary's.'

'Pick up in five minutes. Stay safe.'

The phone was replaced and Fergus was already in the cupboard pulling the emergency kits. It wasn't often that A&E staff had to attend incidents in other places, but all staff were trained for the contingency.

Lachlan's head was spinning. Portobello. Where Iris and Holly lived. He felt sick. 'Fergus, you're with me. Ryan, get kitted up, and, Rena, you're with him.'

The news was apparently already filtering throughout the hospital as a few other doctors from other departments appeared. Lachlan slipped the large jacket on with fluorescent writing saying 'Doctor' across the back of it. He opened the emergency pack and double-checked all the equipment he might need. He grabbed some extra gloves and stuffed them in his pockets.

Fergus appeared beside him with his emergency pack on his shoulder. 'Ready,' he said. He'd changed his normal lower scrubs and was now wearing waterproof trousers and a pair of trainers.

'Done this before?' asked Lachlan.

'Last time was a couple of years ago in a

multicar pile-up in a thunderstorm. Was out there for six hours.'

Lachlan nodded. They walked to entrance and, when the ambulances pulled up, climbed in. 'Any more information?' asked Lachlan as he strapped himself in.

'Could be a gas explosion. Unconfirmed report that people in the area had reported a smell of gas a few hours earlier.'

'Any word about the damage?'

'Fire services are on-site. They say that a whole block of terraced houses is affected. One almost obliterated, two are half-collapsed and a number of others have significant damage.'

'What's the street name?'

The paramedic repeated it and Lachlan sagged back in his seat. He glanced around at Fergus. 'That's Iris's street.'

The two of them sat in silence while the blue-lighted ambulance raced through the dark streets. There was radio chatter. Confirming it was a gas explosion and services were on-site. There was some debate about whether it was safe for staff to assist.

Lachlan wasn't even there and he could feel his blood boil. But the paramedic alongside him rolled his eyes. 'We'll be going in, and so will the fire crews. I'll get you a hard hat and visor, Doc. We won't be leaving patients behind.'

The ambulance turned the corner and pulled to a halt. Fergus and Lachlan jumped out of the rig, and took a moment to survey the damage, as Ryan and Rena jumped out of the other ambulance behind them. The damage was significant. One house looked like barely a shell—the roof was gone, and the side walls had collapsed. The houses on either side seemed to have lost half of themselves, collapsing precariously.

Other houses had damaged roofs. Windows were blown out, and curtains were fluttering in the wind. He could see a few people who had clearly been evacuated from their homes. Some in a state of undress. All shell-shocked.

The Guardai had taken command of the situation. One commander pointed Ryan and Rena towards some people who looked as if they had been hit by flying debris.

'Do we know how many people are in each household?' asked Lachlan.

The commander looked up. 'We're having to go on what the neighbours are telling us right now. Someone from the city will join us shortly with more details.' He pointed to the partially destroyed street. 'Number sixteen, a mother and three kids. Father works away. No one's sure if he's home or not, but his car's not there. Number twelve, a mother and one kid. Number fourteen, elderly couple, adult son and teenage grandson. That's where the focus is right now.'

Twelve. Was number twelve Iris's house? He didn't know for sure. He walked swiftly over to where he could see some of the neighbours gathered together. 'Excuse me, can I check? One of my colleagues stays in this street. Iris Conway, do any of you know her?'

The first couple shook their head. But another woman frowned. 'Is that Holly's mum?'

'Yes, yes, it is.'

The woman's eyes were filled with tears. 'Yes, that's their house over there.'

She pointed to one of the half-collapsed houses and Lachlan felt his stomach heave. 'Thank you,' he said, before making his way over the fire and rescue crews and grabbing a hard hat and visor for himself and Fergus. 'Do you have anyone you need me to treat right now?' he asked.

He could see a variety of rescue crew in bright clothing dotted amongst the debris. Some attempts had been made to try and make these buildings safe, with walls propped, but all the staff working here would know there were risks involved.

Lachlan had a job to do. He was happy to take those risks.

'We need a doc here?' A hand waved and Lachlan and Fergus ran over.

'I've got someone trapped under some rubble. Need to check it's safe to move them.'

Fergus glanced around. 'Want me to take this one?'

Lachlan hesitated. What he really wanted to do was wade into the rubble that was Iris's house and start heaving bricks out of the way, and try to find either her or Holly. But he knew that was crazy. He knew he had to let the other services do their part of the job first.

'We'll do it together,' he said to Fergus, and they made their way over. It was the older man, and he was pinned partly beneath a piece of furniture that a wall had subsequently collapsed on. Lachlan and Fergus took some time to stabilise him, check for any other issues, then gently eased him out as the fire crew relieved the weight by just a few inches. He was transferred quickly onto a stretcher and back to the main hub where Ryan and Rena would take care of him.

'Doc.' Another shout. This time it was Iris's house. 'I've got a kid trapped. Not sure if she's injured. She won't talk to me.'

Lachlan sprinted over, his heart leaping in all sorts of ways, making his way over unstable rubble and family items. Toys, kitchenware, a set of yellow curtains. His insides were roiling over and over. These were Iris's things, Holly's things. Things belonging to living, breathing people that he knew.

He put his hand on the shoulder of the rescue worker. The guy looked up. 'I've got a kid down here. Through the gap. I think she's under a kitchen table. Right now, the only way out is through this gap. But I can't persuade her. Can you try?'

Lachlan dropped to his knees. 'This little girl was caught up in the train accident just a couple of weeks ago. She might be having flashbacks. Let me see what I can do.'

'Sure, Doc. I'll be right behind you. Let me know what I can do. Poor kid.'

Lachlan pressed his face toward the thinnish gap. It took his eyes a few seconds to adjust to the dimness. He turned to the guy. 'Do you have something I could use to pass something down to her?'

The guy nodded. 'Give me a sec.'

Lachlan took a deep breath. 'Holly, this is Lachlan. I'm one of the doctors that works with your mum. Can you hear me?'

There was sniffing, but no real answer.

'Holly, I'm here to help you. I'm here to help your mum. Can you let me know if you're hurt at all? Or if you're stuck?'

There was a tap on his shoulder, and the rescue worker handed him a long rod with a pincer at the end. Perfect.

Lachlan wrestled his phone out of his pocket. He could only begin to imagine how scared Holly was. He flicked on the torch on his phone and disabled his fingerprint status, then he put it in the pincer. 'Holly, I'm going to send down my phone to you, so you will be able to see a bit better. The torch is already switched on, so it might dazzle you for a second as it comes down. Okay?'

There was a murmur that sounded like *okay*.

He, ever so slowly, sent the rod down the thin gap with the phone going first. When he was sure it had reached her, he shouted some instructions. 'Holly, grab the phone. Can you reach it?'

He felt the movement before he heard anything. 'Got it,' was the small reply.

Lachlan breathed a sigh of relief. 'Okay, honey. Give yourself a minute. I think you might be trapped under the kitchen table. Can you tell me if that's right?'

'Ye…es,' came the wobbly answer.

'Okay, are you there yourself, or is anyone there with you?' His chest felt tight as he asked the question.

'Just me…'

His heart sank, but he focused on what he needed to do. 'Okay. Are you hurt anywhere, Holly?'

'No...'

'Good. Can you move about okay?'

'Yes, but there's not much room. And it's creaky.'

Lachlan quelled his panic, thinking the table was likely creaking under the strain of the weight on top of it. 'Great. Do you think you could get through this space and come out to me?'

There was silence, before finally, 'I don't know you.'

Lachlan did his best to put himself into Holly's point of view. 'Okay, do you remember meeting me at the hospital with your mum after the accident?'

'Maybe.'

'Well, your mum would want me to make sure you're safe. Only way I can do that is if you can get through this space to me. Can you do that?'

The silence lasted for ever. She was scared. 'Is my mum there?'

Lachlan bit his bottom lip and wondered if he should lie. Truth was, he had no idea where Iris was, or if she was still alive. Every part of him wanted to throw this building apart to find her, but he knew he had to prioritise Holly. That was what Iris would want him to do. He could do that for her.

Something came into his head. 'Holly, do you know how to work those phones?'

'Yes.'

'Okay. Find the app for the photos. If you can do it, look right back at the beginning.'

He held his breath. Would she notice he hadn't answered the question about her mum?

'Have you done it?'

There was a little gasp. 'Is that my mum?'

He sighed. 'Yes, it is. We knew each other years ago. There's just a couple of photos. But I want you to know that your mum and I have been friends for a long time. You're safe with me.'

'She's laughing,' said Holly. 'You're laughing.'

'We used to do that a lot.'

There was a signal from behind him. Fergus. He bent forward and spoke in a low voice. 'It's Iris. They've found her.'

'Is she alive?' Lachlan mouthed the words so Holly would have no chance of hearing them. Every muscle in his body was tense right now. All he wanted to know was that she was alive. If she was injured, he could help. No matter what had happened to her. If she needed care—

he would do it. All he wanted to do was help the woman that he loved. He'd been a fool. He'd seen the fact that Iris had moved on with her life in a real, positive way yet he hadn't listened properly to everything she'd been telling him. He'd been so wrapped up in what he thought was her deceit that he couldn't see the bigger picture.

Fergus gave a nod, and Lachlan's heart soared. 'Give me five,' he mouthed, and turned his full concentration on getting Holly out.

It took some coaching and reassurance. But Holly finally squeezed her way through the hole that had been made. As soon as she was within arm's reach, Lachlan gently lifted her the rest of the way, talking the whole time. He gave her a quick check over. She turned the phone towards him and he looked at the picture she'd kept on the screen.

It was ancient. Iris and Lachlan were sitting on the grass together in Kensington Gardens in London with the swan pond in the distance. They were laughing at something a friend had said and the moment had been captured perfectly on camera. It was an old photo that Lachlan had scanned digitally years ago. It had been in amongst his digital storage and he hadn't looked at it, or the other few that he had, in years.

Seeing them back then tore at his heart. 'You look so happy,' Holly said with a wistful tone in her voice.

'We were.'

'But you're not happy now.'

Lachlan stiffened. 'What do you mean?'

'Mum told me she upset you and she was sad.' Holly swivelled her head from side to side. 'Where is she?'

She'd been sheltered from this. She likely hadn't understood that the gas blast had almost destroyed her family home. She started to shake, and he wrapped his arms around her and carried her away from the area. 'I'm just going to see your mum now, Holly. As soon as I've checked her, I'll make sure you can see each other. But I'm taking to you Rena now, and she will look after you while I'm getting your mum.'

Holly looked at him again. 'You're not upset now?'

It was an odd question for a child whose house had just disintegrated around her to ask. But children had many different coping mechanisms, and Lachlan figured that, right now, thinking about this instead of anything else was Holly's. He gave her the most reassuring smile that he could. 'I'm not upset with your

mum now, Holly. I promise. This is nothing
that can't be fixed.'

He walked over to the temporary aid station
that had been set up, and Rena gave a shout of
glee when she saw Holly, rushing over to get
her. Lachlan gladly handed her over and made
his way back to the partially collapsed building to find Fergus.

'Here, Doc!' He saw the wave of Fergus's
hand as he picked his way through the debris.
Iris was pinned underneath rubble, her hair
covered in dust and only one arm visible. Three
rescue crew were working around her, trying to
find the best way to extricate her safely.

Fergus had already put an oximeter on her
finger, and an oxygen mask on her face. He'd
used scissors to cut the sleeve on Iris's top, to
reveal her arm properly. 'Was just going to get
some IV access. Want to take over?'

'Gladly,' said Lachlan, sliding into the space
that Fergus vacated.

He could see at a glance that Iris's oxygen
levels were slightly lower than normal. He slid
a needle into her arm quickly, inserting the
cannula and securing it, before checking her
blood pressure. Low. She could have other injuries. By the time he looked up, Fergus had
already run some IV fluids through a line and
was holding it out to him.

He fastened it quickly and put his head down next to Iris's. He reached out and touched her face. 'Iris, Iris, it's Lachlan. There's been a gas explosion. I'm here to help.'

There was a faint groan as he stroked the side of her face. Her eyelids flickered. She automatically tried to move her body and let out a sharp yelp of pain. 'Holly,' she breathed. 'Holly.'

'I've got her, Iris. She's safe. We're just going to find a way to get you out too.'

She started to become more alert. 'Lachlan?' She looked confused, as if she didn't really believe what she was seeing.

'Yes,' he said. 'I'm here. So is some of the team.'

'What happened?' she blinked again.

'There was a gas explosion. Took out some of the houses in the street.'

'That smell,' she groaned, turning her head to the side. It was as if she realised she was trapped. She tried to sit up but couldn't. 'Lachlan?' There was panic in her voice.

He took her hand. 'It'll be okay, Iris. The rescue crew are going to find a way to get you out. Till they do, I'll be here. And Holly is safe with Rena.'

Iris took a few stuttered breaths. 'Can't move, can't breathe,' she gasped. She tried to pull the mask from her face.

'No, leave it, you need it right now,' he ordered.

'Move, Doc,' came the order from behind him. He turned to see the fire and rescue crew with equipment that looked as if it might take some of the weight to allow Iris to be pulled out.

Another crew member appeared with an orange flexible sliding board. It was clear they were going to try and get it under Iris, to try and get her out quickly as soon as the weight was lifted.

Fergus didn't even need an instruction. He picked his away around the rubble to assist at the other side.

'Iris, we're getting you out. Fergus is at your other side. The crew are going to try and slide something under you. Can you lift your back at all?'

She gave a cough. 'Yes, a little. I can lift my shoulders.'

Fergus gave a thumbs-up. 'Perfect, just a little more shuffling and we'll be ready.'

Lachlan glanced around, watching everyone prepare. *Please let this work.* All he wanted was to get her out safely.

Lachlan couldn't help himself. He took Iris's hand and squeezed it.

A few moments later there was a commanding shout. 'Ready? We're doing one, two, three and pull.'

There were shouts of assent all round and the lead fire and rescue officer shouted clearly. 'One, two, three, *pull*!'

There was some loud creaking, a waft of dust, and Iris was pulled out. She was pale and looked shell-shocked. Lachlan let go of her hand and grabbed one of the handholds in the sliding board. The rescue crew all picked their way across the rubble and over to the emergency tent.

Iris was moved onto a nearby trolley and Lachlan grabbed his stethoscope, leaning over her and touching her face. 'Let's see what we can do to make you feel better.'

'Let me sit up,' she said. She pulled the mask from her face and took some deep breaths, choking a bit.

He was scanning her whole body, assessing everything. There didn't appear to be any obvious injuries.

'Mum!' Holly came running in, and Iris gave a little cry of relief. They hugged and kissed, as Lachlan stood to one side. Fergus stood smiling at the entranceway.

'You're safe,' Iris kept repeating as she hugged her daughter.

Holly's eyes flickered to Lachlan. 'Your friend helped me,' she said.

Iris looked over at Lachlan and gave him a nod. After she'd examined her daughter from head to foot, Fergus took a step inside, clearly sensing the vibe. 'All right if I go and find Holly something to eat and drink?' He held his hand out to Holly.

Iris glanced at Lachlan, then gave Fergus a grateful smile, dropping another kiss on Holly's head. 'Thanks, Fergus. I'll come and get you in a few minutes,' she said to her daughter, who left quite happily with Fergus.

Silence fell between them. All Lachlan could feel right now was an overwhelming sense of relief that both Iris and Holly were safe.

After a few moments, Iris gave a weak cough, then looked him clean in the eye. 'Why you, Lachlan? Why are you here?' There was a hint of confusion in her voice.

He didn't hesitate. 'Because I knew it was your area. I wanted to make sure you and Holly were safe.'

Her eyes blinked again and she kept staring straight at him. 'But why?'

'Because I love you, Iris. I always have. And I'm going to stay right by your side.'

She took a deep breath and her eyes widened. 'You hate me,' she said simply.

He put his hand on her shoulder and shook his head. 'I love you. It's always been you, Iris. No one else has ever come close. I just reacted badly when you told me everything, and I'm sorry. But you have no idea the wave of fear that came over me when I thought something might have happened to you just now. I couldn't bear that. Not for you, and not for Holly.'

'You helped my daughter,' she sighed.

'And I'd do it again in a heartbeat.'

He took both her hands in his. 'Iris, I know that what happened in our marriage was also my fault. Deep down, I knew there were issues we needed to grapple with, and I didn't try hard enough to work with you on them. I should have made you sit down and talk to me about it. But I didn't. At twenty-three, maybe we were too young to be married. We certainly made a mistake rushing into trying for a family—' he put his hand on his chest '—and I take equal responsibility for that. What I want—' he took a deep breath '—and what I hope you also want, is for us to sit down together and find a way to make things work. I'm not letting you slip through my fingers once again. We're going to fight for this, Iris. We're going to fight for this together.'

He could see she was blinking back tears. 'But what if we argue? What if we still struggle?'

'Then we'll work it out together,' he said firmly. 'I love you, Iris. Nothing is going to change that. This is it. We're older, and I hope we're much wiser. I don't want to lose this chance. Fate put us back together again for a reason, Iris.' He smiled at her. 'We can do this. I have faith.'

She closed her eyes for a second. 'What about Holly?'

'Holly is your daughter. Holly comes first. We'll take things at a pace that suits her.'

He pulled her close to him and dropped a kiss on her forehead. 'We can do this,' he vowed again.

Her face crumpled and she raised her dust-covered face to his. 'Promise me,' she whispered fiercely. 'Promise me we will get through this together. Because I love you too.'

He didn't hesitate for a second. 'Now, and always.'

EPILOGUE

Two years later

'READY?' LACHLAN ASKED. He was standing behind Iris as she checked herself in the full-length mirror one more time.

She spun around, her hair in long curls and her knee-length wedding dress flowing out as she turned. She lifted her hands, one clutching her orange-flowered wedding bouquet, and wrapped them around his neck.

'You look quite handsome today.' She smiled. 'Going somewhere special?'

She'd never looked so beautiful. 'I'm going to get married to a mysterious woman who has stolen my heart not just once, but twice,' he said as bent down to kiss her.

'Taxis are here!' shouted Maeve.

She was standing at the doorway of the extended and newly refurbished cottage that Lachlan, Iris and Holly were now calling their

254 MARRIAGE MIRACLE IN EMERGENCY

home. Although Iris's home had been rebuilt, they'd both decided that the cottage would be a new start for them all, so they'd sold it.

Holly was dressed in a bridesmaid dress of her own choice, with matching flowers in her hair. She had something in her hand. 'Mail,' she said.

Iris and Lachlan froze. They'd been waiting for something and had been anxiously checking the mail for the last week. The envelope was official, white with a blue insignia.

'Let's leave it until after the wedding,' said Iris nervously. 'Just in case it's bad news.'

Lachlan hesitated, then gave his wife-to-be a smile. 'Have confidence,' he said as he took the envelope from Holly's hand and pulled it open.

As he slid the letter from the envelope, he knew everyone else in the household was holding their breath. There was only one word he needed to say. 'Approved!'

'Yes!' shouted Holly. 'I get a brother or a sister.' She was jumping up and down.

Iris had taken the crumpled paper out of Lachlan's hand, and kept scanning it for a second. 'How about both?' she said, beaming from ear to ear. 'We've been matched with twins!'

'Twins?' Lachlan's mouth fell open, and then he started laughing. He picked up Iris with one arm and Holly with the other and swung them both around.

The taxi tooted loudly outside. 'Dublin City Hall is calling!' said Maeve. Scout gave a bark, turning his head to try and gnaw on the bow that had been tied around his neck. 'Let's go, people. Honestly, you two will be late for your own wedding!'

Maeve, Scout and Holly climbed into the black taxi with a bright orange ribbon that matched Holly's dress, and Lachlan and Iris climbed into the other adorned with a cream ribbon.

She snuggled into his side as the taxi started down the lane. 'I'm going to get make-up all over your handsome suit,' she sighed.

'And hopefully lipstick all over my face,' he replied, smiling.

She sat more upright and turned to face him with a broad smile on her face and her eyes gleaming mischievously. 'I don't think we should wait until the ceremony. I think I still need some convincing.'

Lachlan moved too, and settled his hands around her waist. 'That sounds like a good idea to me.' He grinned. 'I think we should definitely get some practice in.'

And so, the bride and groom, both slightly

dishevelled, arrived at Dublin City Hall to the cheers of their friends and walked hand in hand up the steps to start their new life together.

* * * * *

If you enjoyed this story, check out these other great reads from Scarlet Wilson

A Festive Fling in Stockholm
Reawakened by the Italian Surgeon
His Blind Date Bride
Family for the Children's Doc

All available now!